Tubal Cain

Joseph Hergesheimer

Alpha Editions

This edition published in 2024

ISBN : 9789362517272

Design and Setting By
Alpha Editions
www.alphaedis.com
Email - info@alphaedis.com

As per information held with us this book is in Public Domain.
This book is a reproduction of an important historical work. Alpha Editions uses the best technology to reproduce historical work in the same manner it was first published to preserve its original nature. Any marks or number seen are left intentionally to preserve its true form.

Contents

I	- 1 -
II	- 7 -
III	- 14 -
IV	- 26 -
V	- 29 -
VI	- 32 -
VII	- 36 -
VIII	- 42 -
IX	- 46 -
X	- 48 -
XI	- 52 -
XII	- 55 -
XIII	- 61 -
XIV	- 66 -
XV	- 69 -
XVI	- 72 -

I

ALEXANDER HULINGS sat at the dingy, green-baize covered table, with one slight knee hung loosely over the other, and his tenuous fingers lightly gripping the time-polished wooden arms of a hickory chair. He was staring somberly, with an immobile, thin, dark countenance, at the white plaster wall before him. Close by his right shoulder a window opened on a tranquil street, where the vermilion maple buds were splitting; and beyond the window a door was ajar on a plank sidewalk. Some shelves held crumbling yellow calf-bound volumes, a few new, with glazed black labels; at the back was a small cannon stove, with an elbow of pipe let into the plaster; a large steel engraving of Chief Justice Marshall hung on the wall; and in a farther corner a careless pile of paper, folded in dockets or tied with casual string, was collecting a grey film of neglect A small banjo clock, with a brass-railed pediment and an elongated picture in color of the Exchange at Manchester, traced the regular, monotonous passage of minutes into hour.

The hour extended, doubled; but Alexander Hulings barely shifted a knee, a hand. At times a slight convulsive shudder passed through his shoulders, but without affecting his position or the concentrated gloom. Occasionally he swallowed dryly; his grip momentarily tightened on the chair, but his gaze was level. The afternoon waned; a sweet breath of flowering magnolia drifted in at the door; the light grew tender; and footfalls without sounded far away. Suddenly Hulings moved: his chair scraped harshly over the bare floor and he strode abruptly outside, where he stood facing a small tin sign nailed near the door. It read:

ALEXANDER HULINGS

COUNSELOR AT LAW

With a violent gesture, unpremeditated even by himself, he forced his hand under an edge of the sign and ripped it from its place. Then he went back and flung it bitterly, with a crumpling impact, away from him, and resumed his place at the table.

It was the end of that! He had practiced law seven, nine, years, detesting its circuitous trivialities, uniformly failing to establish a professional success, without realizing his utter legal unfitness. Before him on a scrap of paper were the figures of his past year's activities. He had made something over nine hundred dollars. And he was thirty-four years old! Those facts, seen together, dinned failure in his brain. There were absolutely no indications of a brighter future. Two other actualities added to the gloom of his thoughts: one was Hallie Flower; that would have to be encountered at once, this evening; and the other was—his health.

He was reluctant to admit any question of the latter; he had the feeling, almost a superstition, that such an admission enlarged whatever, if anything, was the matter with him. It was vague, but increasingly disturbing; he had described it with difficulty to Doctor Veneada, his only intimate among the Eastlake men, as a sensation like that a fiddlestring might experience when tightened remorselessly by a blundering hand.

"At any minute," he had said, "the damned thing must go!"

Veneada had frowned out of his whiskers.

"What you need," the doctor had decided, "is a complete change. You are strung up. Go away. Forget the law for two or three months. The Mineral is the place for you."

Alexander Hulings couldn't afford a month or more at the Mineral Spring; and he had said so with the sharpness that was one of the annoying symptoms of his condition. He had had several letters, though, throughout a number of years, from James Claypole, a cousin of his mother, asking him out to Tubal Cain, the iron forge which barely kept Claypole alive; and he might manage that—if it were not for Hallie Flower. There the conversation had come to an inevitable conclusion.

Now, in a flurry of violence that was, nevertheless, the expression of complete purpose, he had ended his practice, his only livelihood; and that would—must—end Hallie.

He had been engaged to her from the day when, together, they had, with a pretense of formality, opened his office in Eastlake. He had determined not to marry until he made a thousand dollars in a year; and, as year after year slipped by without his accumulating that amount, their engagement had come to resemble the unemotional contact of a union without sex. Lately Hallie had seemed almost content with duties in her parental home and the three evenings weekly that Alexander spent with her in the formal propriety of a front room.

His own feelings defied analysis; but it seemed to him that, frankly surveyed, even his love for Hallie Flower had been swallowed up in the tide of irritability rising about him. He felt no active sorrow at the knowledge that he was about to relinquish all claim upon her; his pride stirred resentfully; the evening promised to be uncomfortable—but that was all.

The room swam about him in a manner that had grown hatefully familiar; he swayed in his chair; and his hands were at once numb with cold and wet with perspiration. A sinking fear fastened on him, an inchoate dread that he fought bitterly. It wasn't death from which Alexander Hulings shuddered, but a crawling sensation that turned his knees to dust. He was a slight man, with narrow shoulders and close-swinging arms, but as rigidly erect as an iron bar; his mentality was like that too, and he particularly detested the variety of nerves that had settled on him.

A form blocked the doorway, accentuating the dusk that had swiftly gathered in the office, and Veneada entered. His neckcloth was, as always, carelessly folded, and his collar hid in rolls of fat; a cloak was thrown back from a wide girth, and he wore an incongruous pair of buff linen trousers.

"What's this—mooning in the dark?" he demanded. "Thought you hadn't locked the office door. Come out; fill your lungs with the spring and your stomach with supper."

Without reply, Alexander Hulings followed the other into the street.

"I am going to Hallie's," he said in response to Veneada's unspoken query.

Suddenly he felt that he must conclude everything at once and get away; where and from what he didn't know. It was not his evening to see Hallie and she would be surprised when he came up on the step. The Flowers had supper at five; it would be over now, and Hallie finished with the dishes and free. Alexander briefly told Veneada his double decision.

"In a way," the other said, "I'm glad. You must get away for a little anyway; and you are accomplishing nothing here in Eastlake. You are a rotten lawyer, Alexander; any other man would have quit long ago; but your infernal stubbornness held you to it. You are not a small-town man. You see life in a different, a wider way. And if you could only come on something where your pigheadedness counted there's no saying where you'd reach. I'm sorry for Hallie; she's a nice woman, and you could get along well enough on nine hundred——"

"I said I'd never marry until I made a thousand in a year," Hulings broke in, exasperated.

"Good heavens! Don't I know that?" Veneada replied. "And you won't, you—you mule! I guess I've suffered enough from your confounded character to know what it means when you say a thing. I think you're right about this. Go up to that fellow Claypole and show him what brittle stuff iron is compared to yourself. Seriously, Alex, get out and work like the devil at a heavy job; go to bed with your back ruined and your hands raw. You know I'll miss you—means a lot to me, best friend."

A deep embarrassment was visible on Veneada; it was communicated to Alexander Hulings, and he was relieved when they drew opposite the Flowers' dwelling.

It was a narrow, high brick structure, with a portico cap, supported by cast-iron grilling, and shallow iron-railed balconies on the second story. A gravel path divided a small lawn beyond a gate guarded by two stone greyhounds. Hallie emerged from the house with an expression of mild inquiry at his unexpected appearance. She was a year older than himself, an erect, thin woman, with a pale coloring and unstirred blue eyes.

"Why, Alex," she remarked, "whatever brought you here on a Saturday?" They sat, without further immediate speech, from long habit, in familiar chairs.

He wondered how he was going to tell her. And the question, the difficulty, roused in him an astonishing amount of exasperation. He regarded her almost vindictively, with covertly shut hands. He must get hold of himself. Hallie, to whom he was about to do irreparable harm, the kindest woman in existence! But he realized that whatever feeling he had had for her was gone for ever; she had become merged indistinguishably into the thought of East-lake; and every nerve in him demanded a total separation from the slumbrous town that had witnessed his legal failure.

He wasn't, he knew, normal; his intention here was reprehensible, but he was without will to defeat it. Alexander Hulings felt the clumsy hand drawing tighter the string he had pictured himself as being; an overwhelming impulse overtook him to rush away—anywhere, immediately. He said in a rapid blurred voice:

"Hallie, this... our plans are a failure. That is, I am. The law's been no good; I mean, I haven't. Can't get the hang of the—the damned——"

"Alex!" she interrupted, astonished at the expletive.

"I'm going away," he gabbled on, only half conscious of his words in waves of giddy insecurity. "Yes; for good. I'm no use here! Shot to pieces, somehow. Forgive me. Can't get a thousand."

Hallie Flower said in a tone of unpremeditated surprise:

"Then I'll never be married!"

She sat with her hands open in her lap, a wistfulness on her countenance that he found only silly. He cursed himself, his impotence, bitterly. Now he wanted to get away; but there remained an almost more impossible consummation—Hallie's parents. They were old; she was an only child.

"Your father——" he muttered.

On his feet he swayed like a pendulum. Viselike fingers gripped at the back of his neck. The hand of death? Incredibly he lived through a stammering, racking period, in the midst of which a cuckoo ejaculated seven idiotic notes from the fretted face of a clock.

He was on the street again; the cruel pressure was relaxed; he drew a deep breath. In his room, a select chamber with a "private" family, he packed and strapped his small leather trunk. There was nowhere among his belongings a suggestion of any souvenir of the past, anything sentimental or charged with memory. A daguerreotype of Hallie Flower, in an embossed black case lined with red plush, he ground into a shapeless fragment. Afterward he was shocked by what he had done and was forced to seek the support of a chair. He clenched his jaw, gazed with stony eyes against the formless dread about him.

He had forgotten that the next day was Sunday, with a corresponding dislocation of the train and packet service which was to take him West. A further wait until Monday was necessary. Alexander Hulings got through that too; and was finally seated with Veneada in his light wagon, behind a clattering pair of young Hambletonians, with the trunk secured in the rear. Veneada was taking him to a station on the Columbus Railroad. Though the morning had hardly advanced, and Hulings had wrapped himself in a heavy cape, the doctor had only a duster, unbuttoned, on his casual clothing.

"You know, Alex," the latter said—"and let me finish before you start to object—that I have more money than I can use. And, though I know you wouldn't just borrow any for cigars, if there ever comes a time when you need a few thousands, if you happen on something that looks good for both of us, don't fail to let me know. You'll pull out of this depression; I think you're a great man, Alex—because you are so unpleasant, if for nothing else."

The doctor's weighty hand fell affectionately on Hulings' shoulder.

Hulings involuntarily moved from the other's contact; he wanted to leave all—all of Eastlake. Once away, he was certain, his being would clarify, grow more secure. He even neglected to issue a characteristic abrupt refusal of Veneada's implied offer of assistance; though all that he possessed, now strapped in his wallet, was a meager provision for a debilitated man who had cast safety behind him.

The doctor pulled his horses in beside a small, boxlike station, on flat wooden tracks, dominated by a stout pole, to which was nailed a ladderlike succession of cross blocks.

Alexander Hulings was infinitely relieved when the other, after some last professional injunctions, drove away. Already, he thought, he felt better; and he watched, with a faint stirring of normal curiosity, the station master climb the pole and survey the mid-distance for the approaching train.

The engine finally rolled fussily into view, with a lurid black column of smoke pouring from a thin belled stack, and dragging a rocking, precarious brigade of chariot coaches scrolled in bright yellow and staring blue. It stopped, with a fretful ringing and grinding impact of coach on coach. Alexander Hulings' trunk was shouldered to a roof; and after an inspection of the close interiors he followed his baggage to an open seat above. The engine gathered momentum; he was jerked rudely forward and blinded by a cloud of smoke streaked with flaring cinders.

There was a faint cry at his back, and he saw a woman clutching a charring hole in her crinoline. The railroad journey was an insuperable torment; the diminishing crash at the stops, either at a station or where cut wood was stacked to fire the engine, the choking hot waves of smoke, the shouted confabulations between the captain and the engineer, forward on his precarious ledge—all added to an excruciating torture of Hulings' racked and shuddering nerves. His rigid body was thrown from side to side; his spine seemed at the point of splintering from the pounding of the rails.

An utter mental dejection weighed down his shattered being; it was not the past but the future that oppressed him. Perhaps he was going only to die miserably in an obscure hole; Veneada probably wouldn't tell him the truth about his condition. What he most resented, with a tenuous spark of his customary obstinate spirit, was the thought of never justifying a belief he possessed in his ultimate power to conquer circumstance, to be greatly successful.

Veneada, a man without flattery, had himself used that word "great" in connection with him.

Alexander Hulings felt dimly, even now, a sense of cold power; a hunger for struggle different from a petty law practice in Eastlake. He thought of the iron that James Claypole unsuccessfully wrought; and something in the word, its implied obduracy, fired his disintegrating mind. "Iron!" Unconsciously he spoke the word aloud. He was entirely ignorant of what, exactly, it meant, what were the processes of its fluxing and refinement; forge and furnace were hardly separated in his thoughts. But out of the confusion emerged the one concrete stubborn fact—iron!

He was drawn, at last, over a level grassy plain, at the far edge of which evening and clustered houses merged on a silver expanse of river. It was Columbus, where he found the canal packets lying in the terminal-station basin.

II

THE westbound packet, the *Hit or Miss*, started with a long horn blast and the straining of the mules at the towrope. The canal boat slipped into its placid banked waterway. Supper was being laid in the gentlemen's cabin, and Alexander Hulings was unable to secure a berth. The passengers crowded at a single long table; and the low interior, steaming with food, echoing with clattering china and a ceaseless gabble of voices, confused him intolerably. He made his way to the open space at the rear. The soundless, placid movement at once soothed him and was exasperating in its slowness. He thought of his journey as an escape, an emergence from a suffocating cloud; and he raged at its deliberation.

The echoing note of a *cornet-à-piston* sounded from the deck above; it was joined by the rattle of a drum; and an energetic band swept into the strains of Zip Coon. The passengers emerged from supper and gathered on the main deck; the gayly lighted windows streamed in moving yellow bars over dark banks and fields; and they were raised or lowered on the pouring black tide of masoned locks. If it had not been for the infernal persistence of the band, Alexander Hulings would have been almost comfortable; but the music, at midnight, showed no signs of abating. Money was collected, whisky distributed; a quadrille formed forward. Hulings could see the women's crinolines, the great sleeves and skirts, dipping and floating in a radiance of oil torches. He had a place in a solid bank of chairs about the outer rail, and sat huddled in his cape. His misery, as usual, increased with the night; the darkness was streaked with immaterial flashes, disjointed visions. He was infinitely weary, and faint from a hunger that he yet could not satisfy. A consequential male at his side, past middle age, with close whiskers and a mob of seals, addressed a commonplace to him; but he made no reply. The other regarded Hulings with an arrogant surprise, then turned a negligent back. From beyond came a dear, derisive peal of girlish laughter. He heard a name—Gisela—pronounced.

Alexander Hulings' erratic thoughts returned to iron. He wondered vaguely why James Claypole had never succeeded with Tubal Cain. Probably, like so many others, he was a drunkard. The man who had addressed him moved away—he was accompanied by a small party—and another took his vacant place.

"See who that was?" he asked Hulings. The latter shook his head morosely. "Well, that," the first continued impressively, "is John Wooddrop."

Alexander Hulings had an uncertain memory of the name, connected with—

"Yes, sir—John Wooddrop, the Ironmaster. I reckon that man is the biggest—not only the richest but the biggest—man in the state. Thousands of acres, mile after mile; iron banks and furnaces and forges and mills; hundreds of men and women... all his. Like a European monarch! Yes, sir; resembles that. Word's law—says 'Come here!' or 'Go there!' His daughter is with him too, it's clear she's got the old boy's spirit, and his lady. They get off at Harmony; own the valley; own everything about."

Harmony was the place where Hulings was to leave the canal; from there he must drive to Tubal Cain. The vicarious boastfulness of his neighbor stirred within him an inchoate antagonism.

"There is one place near by he doesn't own," he stated sharply.

"Then it's no good," the other promptly replied. "If it was, Wooddrop would have it. It would be his or nothing—he'd see to that. His name is Me, or nobody."

Alexander Hulings' antagonism increased and illogically fastened on the Ironmaster. The other's character, as it had been stated, was precisely the quality that called to the surface his own stubborn will of self-assertion. It precipitated a condition in which he expanded, grew determined, ruthless, cold.

He imagined himself, sick and almost moneyless and bound for Claypole's failure, opposed to John Wooddrop, and got a faint thrill from the fantastic vision. He had a recurrence of the conviction that he, too, was a strong man; and it tormented him with the bitter contrast between such an image and his actual present self. He laughed aloud, a thin, shaken giggle, at his belief persisting in the face of such irrefutable proof of his failure. Nevertheless, it was firmly lodged in him, like a thorn pricking at his dissolution, gathering his scattered faculties into efforts of angry contempt at the laudation of others.

Veneada and Hallie Flower, he realized, were the only intimates he had gathered in a solitary and largely embittered existence. He had no instinctive humanity of feeling, and his observations, colored by his spleen, had not added to a small opinion of man at large. Always feeling himself to be a figure of supreme importance, he had never ceased to chafe at the small aspect he was obliged to exhibit. This mood had grown, through an uncomfortable sense of shame, to a perpetual disparagement of all other triumph and success.

Finally the band ceased its efforts, the oil lights burned dim, and a movement to the cabins proceeded, leaving him on a deserted deck. At last, utterly exhausted, he went below in search of a berth. They hung four deep about the walls, partly curtained, while the floor of the cabin was filled with clothesracks, burdened with a miscellany of outer garments. One place only was empty— under the ceiling; and he made a difficult ascent to the narrow space. Sleep was an impossibility—a storm of hoarse breathing, muttering, and sleepy oaths dinned on his ears. The cabin, closed against the outer air, grew indescribably polluted. Any former torment of mind and body was minor compared to the dragging wakeful hours that followed; a dread of actual insanity seized him.

Almost at the first trace of dawn the cabin was awakened and filled with fragmentary dressing. The deck and bar were occupied by men waiting for the appearance of the feminine passengers from their cabin forward, and breakfast. The day was warm and fine. The packet crossed a turgid river, at the mouths of other canal routes, and entered a wide pastoral valley.

Alexander Hulings sat facing a smaller, various river; at his back was a barrier of mountains, glossy with early laurel and rhododendron. His face was yellow and sunken, and his lips dry. John Wood-drop passed and repassed him, a girl, his daughter Gisela, on his arm. She wore an India muslin dress, wide with crinoline, embroidered in flowers of blue and green worsted, and a flapping rice-straw hat draped in blond lace. Her face was pointed and alert.

Once Hulings caught her glance, and he saw that her eyes seemed black and—and—impertinent.

An air of palpable satisfaction emanated from the Ironmaster. His eyes were dark too; and, more than impertinent, they held for Hulings an intolerable patronage. John Wooddrop's foot trod the deck with a solid authority that increased the sick man's smoldering scorn. At dinner he had an actual encounter with the other. The table was filling rapidly; Alexander Hulings had taken a place when Wooddrop entered with his group and surveyed the seats that remained.

"I am going to ask you," he addressed Hulings in a deep voice, "to move over yonder. That will allow my family to surround me."

A sudden unreasonable determination not to move seized Hulings. He said nothing; he didn't turn his head nor disturb his position. John Wood-drop repeated his request in still more vibrant tones. Hulings did nothing. He was held in a silent rigidity of position.

"You, sir," Wooddrop pronounced loudly, "are deficient in the ordinary courtesies of travel! And note this, Mrs. Wooddrop,"—he turned to his wife—"I shall never again, in spite of Gisela's importunities, move by public conveyance. The presence of individuals like this——"

Alexander Hulings rose and faced the older, infinitely more important man. His sunken eyes blazed with such a feverish passion that the other raised an involuntary palm.

"Individuals," he added, "painfully afflicted." Suddenly Hulings' weakness betrayed him; he collapsed in his chair with a pounding heart and blurred vision. The incident receded, became merged in the resumption of the commonplace clatter of dinner.

Once more on deck, Alexander Hulings was aware that he had appeared both inconsequential and ridiculous, two qualities supremely detestable to his pride; and this added to his bitterness toward the Ironmaster. He determined to extract satisfaction for his humiliation. It was characteristic of Hulings that he saw himself essentially as John Wood-drop's equal; worldly circumstance had no power to impress him; he was superior to the slightest trace of the complacent inferiority exhibited by last night's casual informer.

The day waned monotonously; half dazed with weariness he heard bursts of music; far, meaningless voices; the blowing of the packet horn. He didn't go down again into the cabin to sleep, but stayed wrapped in his cloak in a chair. He slept through the dawn and woke only at the full activity of breakfast. Past noon the boat tied up at Harmony. The Wooddrops departed with all the circumstance of worldly importance and in the stir of cracking whip and restive, spirited horses. Alexander Hulings moved unobserved, with his trunk, to the bank.

Tubal Cain, he discovered, was still fifteen miles distant, and—he had not told James Claypole of his intended arrival—no conveyance was near by. A wagon drawn by six mules with gay bells and colored streamers and heavily loaded with limestone finally appeared, going north, on which Hulings secured passage.

The precarious road followed a wooded ridge, with a vigorous stream on the right and a wall of hills beyond. The valley was largely uninhabited. Once they passed a solid, foursquare structure of stone, built against a hill, with clustered wooden sheds and a great wheel revolving under a smooth arc of water. A delicate white vapor trailed from the top of the masonry, accompanied by rapid, clear flames.

"Blue Lump Furnace," the wagon driver briefly volunteered. "Belongs to Wooddrop. But that doesn't signify anything about here. Pretty near everything's his."

Alexander Hulings looked back, with an involuntary deep interest in the furnace. The word "iron" again vibrated, almost clanged, through his mind. It temporarily obliterated the fact that here was another evidence of the magnitude, the possessions, of John Wooddrop. He was consumed by a sudden anxiety to see James Claypole's forge. Why hadn't the fool persisted, succeeded?

"Tubal Cain's in there." The mules were stopped. "What there is of it! Four bits will be enough."

He was left beside his trunk on the roadside, clouded by the dust of the wagon's departure. Behind him, in the direction indicated, the ground, covered with underbrush, fell away to a glint of water and some obscure structures. Dragging his baggage he made his way down to a long wooden shed, the length facing him open on two covered hearths, some dilapidated troughs, a suspended ponderous hammer resting on an anvil, and a miscellaneous heap of rusting iron implements—long-jawed tongs, hooked rods, sledges, and broken castings. The hearths were cold; there was not a stir of life, of activity, anywhere.

Hulings left his trunk in a clearing and explored farther. Beyond a black heap of charcoal, standing among trees, were two or three small stone dwellings. The first was apparently empty, with some whitened sacks on a bare floor; but within a second he saw through the open doorway the lank figure of a man kneeling in prayer. His foot was on the sill; but the bowed figure, turned away, remained motionless.

Alexander Hulings hesitated, waiting for the prayer to reach a speedy termination. But the other, with upraised, quivering hands, remained so long on his knees that Hulings swung the door back impatiently. Even then an appreciable time elapsed before the man inside rose to his feet. He turned and moved forward, with an abstracted gaze in pale-blue eyes set in a face seamed and scored by time and disease. His expression was benevolent; his voice warm and cordial.

"I am Alexander Hulings," that individual briefly stated; "and I suppose you're Claypole."

The latter's condition, he thought instantaneously, was entirely described by his appearance. James Claypole's person was as neglected as the forge. His stained breeches were engulfed in scarred leather boots, and a coarse black shirt was open on a gaunt chest.

His welcome left nothing to be desired. The dwelling into which he conducted Hulings consisted of a single room, with a small shed kitchen at the rear and two narrow chambers above. There was a pleasant absence of apology for the meager accommodations. James Claypole was an entirely unaffected and simple host.

The late April evening was warm; and after a supper, prepared by Claypole, of thick bacon, potatoes and saleratus biscuit, the two men sat against the outer wall of the house. On the left Hulings could see the end of the forge shed, with the inevitable water wheel hung in a channel cut from the dear stream. The stream wrinkled and whispered along spongy banks, and a flicker hammered on a resonant limb. Hulings stated negligently that he had arrived on the same packet with John Wood-drop, and Claypole retorted:

"A man lost in the world! I tried to wrestle with his spirit, but it was harder than the walls of Jericho."

His eyes glowed with fervor. Hulings regarded him curiously. A religious fanatic! He asked:

"What's been the trouble with Tubal Cain? Other forges appear to flourish about here. This Wooddrop seems to have built a big thing with iron."

"Mammon!" Claypole stated. "Slag; dross! Not this, but the Eternal World." The other failed to comprehend, and he said so irritably. "All that," Claypole specified, waving toward the forge, "takes the thoughts from the Supreme Being. Eager for the Word, and a poor speller-out of the Book, you can't spend priceless hours shingling blooms. And then the men left, one after another, because I stopped pandering to their carnal appetites. No one can indulge in rum here, in a place of mine sealed to God."

"Do you mean that whisky was a part of their pay and that you held it back?" Alexander Hulings demanded curtly. He was without the faintest sympathy for what he termed such arrant folly.

"Yes, just that; a brawling, froward crew. Wooddrop wanted to buy, but I wouldn't extend his wicked dominion, satisfy fleshly lust."

"It's a good forge, then?"

"None better! I built her mostly myself, when I was laying up the treasure that rusted; stone on stone, log on log. Heavy, slow work. The sluice is like a city wall; the anvil bedded on seven feet of oak. It's right! But if I'd known then I should have put up a temple to Jehovah."

Hulings could scarcely contain his impatience.

"Why," he ejaculated, "you might have made a fine thing out of it! Opportunity, opportunity, and you let it go by. For sheer——"

He broke off at a steady gaze from Claypole's calm blue eyes. It was evident that he would have to restrain any injudicious characterizations of the other's belief. He spoke suddenly:

"I came up here because I was sick and had to get out of Eastlake. I left everything but what little money I had. You see—I was a failure. I'd like to stay with you a while; when perhaps I might get on my feet again. I feel easier than I have for weeks." He realized, surprised, that this was so. He had a conviction that he could sleep here, by the stream, in the still, flowering woods. "I haven't any interest in temples," he continued; "but I guess—two men—we won't argue about that. Some allowance on both sides. But I am interested in iron; I'd like to know this forge of yours backward. I've discovered a sort of hankering after the idea; just that—iron. It's a tremendous fact, and you can keep it from rusting."

III

THE following morning Claypole showed Alexander Hulings the mechanics of Tubal Cain. A faint reminiscent pride shone through the later unworldly preoccupation. He lifted the sluice gate, and the water poured through the masoned channel of the forebay and set in motion the wheel, hung with its lower paddles in the course. In the forge shed Claypole bound a connection, and the short haft of the trip hammer, caught in revolving cogs, raised a ponderous head and dropped it, with a jarring clang, on the anvil. The blast of the hearths was driven by water wind, propelled by a piston in a wood cylinder, with an air chamber for even pressure. It was all so elemental that the neglect of the last years had but spread over the forge an appearance of ill repair. Actually it was as sound as the clear oak largely used in its construction.

James Claypole's interest soon faded; he returned to his chair by the door of the dwelling, where he laboriously spelled out the periods of a battered copy of Addison's "Evidences of the Christian Religion." He broke the perusal with frequent ecstatic ejaculations; and when Hulings reluctantly returned from his study of the forge the other was again on his knees, lost in passionate prayer. Hulings grew hungry—Claypole was utterly lost in visions—cooked some bacon and found cold biscuit in the shedlike kitchen.

The afternoon passed into a tenderly fragrant twilight The forge retreated, apparently through the trees, into the evening. Alexander Hulings sat regarding it with an increasing impatience; first, it annoyed him to see such a potentiality of power lying fallow, and then his annoyance ripened into an impatience with Claypole that he could scarcely contain. The impracticable ass! It was a crime to keep the wheel stationary, the hearths cold.

He had a sudden burning desire to see Tubal Cain stirring with life; to hear the beat of the hammer forging iron; to see the dark, still interior lurid with fire. He thought again of John Wooddrop, and his instinctive disparagement of the accomplishments of others mocked both them and himself. If he, Alexander Hulings, had had Claypole's chance, his beginning, he would be more powerful than Wooddrop now.

The law was a trivial foolery compared to the fashioning, out of the earth itself, of iron. Iron, the indispensable! Railroads, in spite of the popular, vulgar disbelief, were a coming great factor; a thousand new uses, refinements, improved processes of manufacture were bound to develop. His thoughts took fire and swept over him in a conflagration of enthusiasm. By heaven, if Claypole had failed he would succeed. He, too, would be an Ironmaster!

A brutal chill overtook him with the night; he shook pitiably; dark fears crept like noxious beetles among his thoughts. James Claypole sat, with his hands on his gaunt knees, gazing, it might be, at a miraculous golden city beyond the black curtain of the world. Later Hulings lay on a couch of boards, folded in coarse blankets and his cape, fighting the familiar evil sinking of his oppressed spirit. He was again cold and yet drenched with sweat... if he were defeated now, he thought, if he collapsed, he was done, shattered! And in his swirling mental anguish he clung to one stable, cool fact; he saw, like Claypole, a vision; but not gold—great shadowy masses of iron. Before dawn the dread receded; he fell asleep.

He questioned his companion at breakfast about the details of forging.

"The secret," the latter stated, "is—timber; wood, charcoal. It's bound to turn up; fuel famine will come, unless it is provided against. That's where John Wooddrop's light. He counts on getting it as he goes. A furnace'll burn five or six thousand cords of wood every little while, and that means two hundred or more acres. Back of Harmony, here, are miles of timber the old man won't loose up right for. He calculates no one else can profit with them and takes his own time."

"What does Wooddrop own in the valleys?"

"Well—there's Sally Furnace; the Poole Sawmill tract; the Medlar Forge and Blue Lump; the coal holes on Allen Mountain; Marta Furnace and Reeba Furnace—they ain't right hereabouts; the Lode Orebank; the Blossom Furnace and Charming Forges; Middle and Low Green Forges; the Auspàcher Farm——"

"That will do," Hulings interrupted him moodily; "I'm not an assessor."

Envy lashed his determination to surprising heights. Claypole grew uncommunicative, except for vague references to the Kingdom at hand and the dross of carnal desire. Finally, without a preparatory word, he strode away and disappeared over the rise toward the road. At supper he had not returned; there was no trace of him when, inundated with sleep, Hulings shut the dwelling for the night. All the following day Alexander Hulings expected his host; he spent the hours avidly studying the implements of forging; but the other did not appear. Neither did he the next day, nor the next.

Hulings, surprisingly happy, was entirely alone but for the hidden passage of wagons on the road and the multitudinous birds that inhabited the stream's edge, in the peaceful, increasing warmth of the days and nights. His condition slowly improved. He bought supplies at the packet station on the canal and shortly became as proficient at the stove as James Claypole. Through the day he sat in the mild sunlight or speculated among the implements of the forge. He visualized the process of iron making; the rough pigs, there were sows, too, he had gathered, lying outside the shed had come from the furnace. These were put into the hearths and melted, stirred perhaps; then—what were the wooden troughs for?—hammered, wrought on the anvil. Outside were other irregularly round pieces of iron, palpably closer in texture than the pig. The forging of them, he was certain, had been completed. There were, also, heavy bars, three feet in length, squared at each end.

Everything had been dropped apparently at the moment of James Claypole's absorbing view of another, transcending existence. Late in an afternoon—it was May—he heard footfalls descending from the road; with a sharp, unreasoning regret, he thought the other had returned. But it was a short, ungainly man with a purplish face and impressive shoulders. "Where's Jim?" he asked with a markedly German accent.

Alexander Hulings told him who he was and all he knew about Claypole.

"I'm Conrad Wishon," the newcomer stated, sinking heavily into a chair. "Did Jim speak of me—his head forgeman? No! But I guess he told you how he stopped the schnapps. Ha! James got religion. And he went away two weeks ago? Maybe he'll never be back. This"—he waved toward the forge—"means nothing to him.

"I live twenty miles up the road, and I saw a Glory-wagon coming on—an old Conestoga, with the Bible painted on the canvas, a traveling Shouter slapping the reins, and a congregation of his family staring out the back. James would take up with a thing like that in a shot. Yes, sir; maybe now you will never see him again. And your mother's cousin! There's no other kin I've heard of; and I was with him longer than the rest."

Hulings listened with growing interest to the equable flow of Conrad Wishon's statements and mild surprise.

"Things have been bad with me," the smith continued. "My wife, she died Thursday before breakfast, and one thing and another. A son has charge of a coaling gang on Allen Mountain, but I'm too heavy for that; and I was going down to Green Forge when I thought I'd stop and see Jim. But, hell!—Jim's gone; like as not on the Glory-wagon. I can get a place at any hearth," he declared pridefully. "I'm a good forger; none better in Hamilton County. When it's shingling a loop I can show 'em all!"

"Have some supper," Alexander Hulings offered.

They sat late into the mild night, with the moonlight patterned like a grey carpet at their feet, talking about the smithing of iron. Conrad Wishon revealed the practical grasp of a life capably spent at a single task, and Hulings questioned him with an increasing comprehension.

"If you had money," Wishon explained, "we could do something right here. I'd like to work old Tubal Cain. I understand her."

The other asked: "How much would it take?"

Conrad Wishon spread out his hands hopelessly. "A lot; and then a creekful back of that! Soon as Wooddrop heard the hammer trip, he'd be around to close you down. Do it in a hundred ways—no teaming principally."

Hillings' antagonism to John Wooddrop increased perceptibly; he became obsessed by the fantastic thought of founding himself—Tubal Cain—triumphantly in the face of the established opposition. But he had nothing—no money, knowledge, or even a robust person. Yet his will to succeed in the valleys hardened into a concrete aim.... Conrad Wishon would be invaluable.

The latter stayed through the night and even lingered, after breakfast, into the morning. He was reluctant to leave the familiar scene of long toil. They were sitting lost in discussion when the beat of horses' hoofs was arrested on the road, and a snapping of underbrush announced the appearance of a young man with a keen, authoritative countenance.

"Mr. James Claypole?" he asked, addressing them collectively.

Alexander Hulings explained what he could of Claypole's absence.

"It probably doesn't matter," the other returned. "I was told the forge wasn't run, for some foolishness or other." He turned to go.

"What did you want with him—with Tubal Cain?" Conrad Wishon asked.

"Twenty-five tons of blooms."

"Now if this was ten years back——"

The young man interrupted the smith, with a gesture of impatience, and turned to go. Hulings asked Conrad Wishon swiftly:

"Could it be done here? Could the men be got? And what would it cost?"

"It could," said Wishon; "they might, and a thousand dollars would perhaps see it through." Hulings sharply called the retreating figure back. "Something more about this twenty-five tons," he demanded.

"For the Penn Rolling Mills," the other crisply replied. "We're asking for delivery in five weeks, but that might be extended a little—at, of course, a loss on the ton. The quality must be first grade."

Wishon grunted.

"Young man," he said, "blooms I made would hardly need blistering to be called steel."

"I'm Philip Grere," the newcomer stated, "of Grere Brothers, and they're the Penn Rolling Mills. We want good blooms soon as possible and it seems there's almost none loose. If you can talk iron, immediate iron, let's get it on paper; if not, I have a long way to drive."

When he had gone Conrad Wishon sat staring, with mingled astonishment and admiration, at Hulings.

"But," he protested, "you don't know nothing about it!"

"You do!" Alexander Hulings told him; he saw himself as a mind, of which Wishon formed the trained and powerful body.

"Perhaps Jim will come back," the elder man continued.

"That is a possibility," Alexander admitted. "But I am going to put every dollar I own into the chance of finishing those twenty-five tons."

The smith persisted: "But you don't know me; perhaps I'm a rascal and can't tell a puddling furnace from a chafery."

Hulings regarded him shrewdly.

"Conrad," he demanded, "can Tubal Cain do it?"

"By Goff," Wishon exclaimed, "she can!"

After an hour of close calculation Conrad Wishon rose with surprising agility.

"I've got enough to do besides sitting here. Tubal Cain ought to have twenty men, anyhow; perhaps I can get eight. There's Mathias Slough, a good hammerman. He broke an elbow at Charming, and Wooddrop won't have him back; but he can work still. Hance, a good nigger, is at my place, and there is another—Surrie. Haines Zer-bey, too, worked at refining, but you'll need to watch his rum. Perhaps Old Man Boeshore will lend a hand, and he's got a strapping grandson—Emanuel. Jeremiah Stell doesn't know much, but he'd let you cut a finger off for a dollar." He shook his head gravely. "That is a middling poor collection."

Alexander Hulings felt capable of operating Tubal Cain successfully with a shift of blind paralytics. A conviction of power, of vast capability, possessed him. Suddenly he seemed to have become a part of the world that moved, of its creative energy; he was like a piece of machinery newly connected with the forceful driving whole. Conrad Wishon had promised to return the next day with the men he had enumerated, and Alexander opened the small scattered buildings about the forge. There were, he found, sufficient living provisions for eight or ten men out of a moldering quantity of primitive bed furnishings, rusted tin, and cracked glass. But it was fortunate that the days were steadily growing warmer.

Wishon had directed him to clean out the channel of the forebay, and throughout the latter half of the day he was tearing heavy weeds from the interstices of the stones, laboring in a chill slime that soon completely covered him. He removed heavy rocks, matted dead bushes, banked mud; and after an hour he was cruelly, impossibly weary. He slipped and bruised a shoulder, cut open his cheek; but he impatiently spat out the blood trailing into his mouth, and continued working. His weariness became a hell of acute pain; without manual practice his movements were clumsy; he wasted what strength he had. Yet as his suffering increased he grew only more relentlessly methodical in the execution of his task. He picked out insignificant obstructions, scraped away grass that offered no resistance to the water power. When he had finished, the forebay, striking in at an angle from the stream to the wheel, was meticulously clean.

He stumbled into his dwelling and fell on the bed, almost instantly asleep, without removing a garment, caked with filth; and never stirred until the sun again flooded the room. He cooked and ravenously ate a tremendous breakfast, and then forced himself to walk the dusty miles that lay between Tubal Cain and the canal. His legs seemed to be totally without joints, and his spine felt like a white-hot bar. At the store about which the insignificant village of Harmony clustered he ordered and paid for a great box of supplies, later carried by an obliging teamster and himself to the forge.

Once more there, he addressed himself to digging out the slag that had hardened in the hearths. The lightest bar soon became insuperably ponderous; ouit wabbled in his grasp, evaded his purpose. Vicious tears streamed over his blackened countenance, and he maintained a constant audible flow of bitter invective. But even that arduous task was nearly accomplished when dark overtook him.

He stripped off his garments, dropping them where he stood, by the forge shed, and literally fell forward into the stream. The cold shock largely revived him, and he supped on huge tins of coffee and hard flitch. Immediately after, he dropped asleep as if he had been knocked unconscious by a club.

At mid-morning he heard a rattle of conveyance from the road and his name called. Above he found a wagon, without a top, filled with the sorriest collection of humanity he had ever viewed, and drawn by a dejected bony horse and a small wicked mule.

"Here they are," Conrad Wishon announced; "and Hance brought along his girl to cook."

Mathias Slough, the hammerman, was thin and grey, as if his face were covered with cobwebs; Hance, Conrad's nigger, black as an iron bloom, was carrying upside down a squawking hen; Surrie, lighter, had a dropped jaw and hands that hung below his knees; Haines Zerbey had pale, swimming eyes, and executed a salute with a battered flat beaver hat; Old Man Boeshore resembled a basin, bowed in at the stomach, his mouth sunken on toothless gums, but there was agility in his step; and Emanuel, his grandson, a towering hulk of youth, presented a facial expanse of mingled pimples and down. Jeremiah Stell was a small, shriveled man, with dead-white hair on a smooth, pinkish countenance.

Standing aside from the nondescript assemblage of men and transient garments, Alexander Hulings surveyed them with cold determination; two emotions possessed him—one of an almost humorous dismay at the slack figures on whom so much depended; and a second, stronger conviction that he could force his purpose even from them. They were, in a manner, his first command; his first material from which to build the consequence, the success, that he felt was his true expression.

He addressed a few brief periods to them; and there was no warmth, no effort to conciliate, in his tones, his dry statement of a heavy task for a merely adequate gain. He adopted this attitude instinctively, without forethought; he was dimly conscious, as a principle, that underpaid men were more easily driven than those over-fully rewarded. And he intended to drive the men before him to the limit of their capability. They had no individual existence for Alexander Hulings, no humanity; they were merely the implements of a projection of his own; their names—Haines Zerbey, Slough—had no more significance than the terms bellows or tongs.

They scattered to the few habitations by the stream, structures mostly of logs and plaster; and in a little while there rose the odorous smoke and sputtering fat of Hance's girl's cooking. Conrad Wishon soon started the labor of preparing the forge. Jeremiah Stell, who had some slight knowledge of carpentry, was directed to repair the plunger of the water-wind apparatus. Slough was testing the beat and control of the trip hammer. Hance and Surrie carried outside the neglected heaps of iron hooks and tongs. Conrad explained to Alexander Hulings:

"I sent word to my son about the charcoal; he'll leave it at my place, but we shall have to haul it from there. Need another mule—maybe two. There's enough pig here to start, and my idea is to buy all we will need now at Blue Lump; they'll lend us a sled, so's we will have it in case old Wooddrop tries to clamp down on us. I'll go along this afternoon and see the head furnace man. It will take money."

Without hesitation, Hulings put a considerable part of his entire small capital into the other's hand. At suppertime Conrad Wishon returned with the first load of metal for the Penn Rolling Mills contract.

Later Hance produced a wheezing accordion and, rocking on his feet, drew out long, wailing notes. He sang:

"Brothers, let us leave

Bukra Land for Hayti;

There we be receive

Grand as Lafayette"

"With changes of men," Conrad continued to Alexander Hulings, "the forges could run night and day, like customary. But with only one lot we'll have to sleep. Someone will stay up to tend the fires."

In the morning the labor of making the wrought blooms actually commenced. Conrad Wishon and Hance at one hearth, and Haines Zerbey with Sur-rie at the other, stood ceaselessly stirring, with long iron rods, the fluxing metal at the incandescent cores of the fires. Alexander then saw that the troughs of water were to cool the rapidly heating rods. Conrad Wishon was relentless in his insistence on long working of the iron. There were, already, muttered protests. "The dam' stuff was cooked an hour back!" But he drowned the objections in a surprising torrent of German-American cursing.

Hulings was outside the shed when he heard the first dull fall of the hammer; and it seemed to him that the sound had come from a sudden pounding of his expanded heart. He, Alexander Hulings, was making iron; his determination, his capability and will were hammering out of the stubborn raw material of earth a foothold for himself and a justification! The smoke, pouring blackly, streaked with crimson sparks, from the forge shed, sifted a fine soot on the green-white flowers of a dogwood tree. A metallic clamor rose; and Emanuel, the youth, stripped to the waist and already smeared with sweat and grime, came out for a gulping breath of unsullied air.

The characteristics of the small force soon became evident. Conrad Wishon labored ceaselessly, with an unimpaired power at fifty apparent even to Alexander's intense self-absorption. Of the others, Hance, the negro, was easily the superior; his strength was Herculean, his willingness inexhaustible. Surrie was sullen. Mathias Slough constantly grumbled at the meager provisions for his comfort and efforts; yet he was a skillful workman. When Alexander had correctly gauged Zer-bey's daily dram he, too, was useful; but the others were negligible. They made the motions of labor, but force was absent.

Alexander Hulings watched with narrowed eyes. When he was present the work in the shed notably improved; all the men except Conrad avoided his implacable gaze. He rarely addressed a remark to them; he seemed withdrawn from the operation that held so much for him. Conrad Wishon easily established his dexterity at "shingling a loop."

Working off a part of a melting sow, he secured it with wide-jawed shingling tongs; and, steadying the pulsating mass on an iron plate, he sledged it into a bloom. For ten hours daily the work continued, the hearths burned, the trip hammer fell and fell. The interior of the shed was a grimy shadow lighted with lurid flares and rose and gentian flowers of iron. Ruddy reflections slid over glistening shoulders and intent, bitter faces; harsh directions, voices, sounded like the grating of castings.

The oddly assorted team was dispatched for charcoal, and then sent with a load of blooms to the canal. Hance had to be spared, with Surrie, for that; the forge was short of labor, and Alexander Hulings joined Conrad in the working of the metal. It was, he found, exhausting toil. He was light and unskilled, and the mass on the hearth slipped continually from his stirring; or else it fastened, with a seeming spite, on his rod, and he was powerless to move it. Often he swung from his feet, straining in supreme, wrenching effort. His body burned with fatigue, his eyes were scorched by the heat of the fires; he lost count of days and nights: They merged imperceptibly one into another; he must have dreamed of his racking exertions, for apparently they never ceased.

Alexander became indistinguishable from the others; all cleanness was forgotten; he ate in a stupefaction of weariness, securing with his fingers whatever was put before him. He was engaged in a struggle the end of which was hidden in the black smoke perpetually hanging over him; in the torment of the present, an inhuman suffering to which he was bound by a tryannical power outside his control, he lost all consciousness of the future.

The hammerman's injured arm prevented his working for two days, and Alexander Hulings cursed him in a stammering rage, before which the other was shocked and dumb. He drove Old Man Boeshore and his grandson with consideration for neither age nor youth; the elder complained endlessly, tears even slid over his corrugated face; the youth was brutally burned, but Hulings never relaxed his demands.

It was as if they had all been caught in a whirlpool, in which they fought vainly for release—the whirlpool of Alexander Hulings' domination. They whispered together, he heard fragments of intended revolt; but under his cold gaze, his thin, tight lips, they subsided uneasily. It was patent that they were abjectly afraid of him.... The blooms moved in a small but unbroken stream over the road to the canal.

He had neglected to secure other horses or mules; and, while waiting for a load of iron on the rough track broken from the road to the forge, the horse slid to his knees, fell over, dead—the last ounce of effort wrung from his angular frame. The mule, with his ears perpetually laid back and a raised lip, seemed impervious to fatigue; his spirit, his wickedness, persisted in the face of appalling toil. The animal's name, Hulings knew, was Alexander; he overheard Hance explaining this to Old Man Boeshore:

"That mule's bound to be Alexander; ain't nobody but an Alexander work like that mule! He's bad too; he'd lay you cold and go right on about his business."

Old Man Boeshore muttered something excessively bitter about the name Alexander.

"If you sh'd ask me," he stated, "I'd tell you that he ain't human. He's got a red light in his eye, like——"

Hulings gathered that this was not still directed at the mule.

More than half of the order for the Penn Rolling Mills had been executed and lay piled by the canal. He calculated the probable time still required, the amount he would unavoidably lose through the delay of faulty equipment and insufficient labor. If James Claypole came back now, he thought, and attempted interference, he would commit murder. It was evening, and he was seated listlessly, with his chair tipped back against the dwelling he shared with Conrad Wishon. The latter, close by, was bowed forward, his head, with a silvery gleam of faded hair, sunk on his breast. A catbird was whistling an elaborate and poignant song, and the invisible stream passed with a faint, choked whisper.

"We're going to have trouble with that girl of Hance's," Wishon pronounced suddenly; "she has taken to meeting Surrie in the woods. If Hance comes on them there will be wet knives!"

Such mishaps, Alexander Hulings knew, were an acute menace to his success. The crippling or loss of Hance might easily prove fatal to his hopes; the negro, immensely powerful, equable, and willing, was of paramount importance.

"I'll stop that!" he declared. But the trouble developed before he had time to intervene.

He came on the two negroes the following morning, facing each other, with, as Conrad had predicted, drawn knives. Hance stood still; but Sur-rie, with bent knees and the point of his steel almost brushing the grass, moved about the larger man. Hulings at once threw himself between them.

"What damned nonsense's this?" he demanded. "Get back to the team, Hance, and you, Surrie, drop your knife!"

The former was on the point of obeying, when Surrie ran in with a sweeping hand. Alexander Hulings jumped forward in a cold fury and felt a sudden numbing slice across his cheek. He had a dim consciousness of blood smearing his shoulder; but all his energy was directed on the stooped figure falling away from his glittering rage.

"Get out!" he directed in a thin, evil voice. "If you are round here in ten minutes I'll blow a hole through your skull!"

Surrie was immediately absorbed by the underbrush.

Hulings had a long diagonal cut from his brow across and under his ear. It bled profusely, and as his temper receded faintness dimmed his vision. Conrad Wishon blotted the wound with cobwebs; a cloth, soon stained, was bound about Alexander's head, and after dinner he was again in the forge, whipping the flagging efforts of his men with a voice like a thin leather thong. If the labor were delayed, he recognized, the contract would not be filled. The workmen were wearing out, like the horse. He moved young Emanuel to the hauling with Hance, the wagon now drawn by three mules. The hammerman's injured arm had grown inflamed, and he was practically one-handed in his management of the trip hammer.

While carrying a lump of iron to the anvil the staggering, ill-assorted group with the tongs dropped their burden, and stood gazing stupidly at the fallen, glowing mass. They were hardly revived by Hulings' lashing scorn. He had increased Haines Zerbey's daily dram, but the drunkard was now practically useless. Jeremiah Stell contracted an intermittent fever; and, though he still toiled in the pursuit of his coveted wage, he was of doubtful value.

Alexander Hulings' body had become as hard as Conrad's knotted forearm. He ate huge amounts of half-cooked pork, washed hastily down by tin cups of black coffee, and fell into instant slumber when the slightest opportunity offered. His face was matted by an unkempt beard; his hands, the pale hands of an Eastlake lawyer, were black, like Hance's, with palms of leather. He surveyed himself with curious amusement in a broken fragment of looking-glass nailed to the wall; the old Hulings, pursued by inchoate dread, had vanished.... In his place was Alexander Hu-lings, a practical iron man! He repeated the descriptive phrase aloud, with an accent of arrogant pride. Later, with an envelope from the Penn Rolling Mills, he said it again, with even more confidence; he held the pay for the blooms which he had-it seemed in another existence—promised to deliver.

He stood leaning on a tree before the forge; within, Conrad Wishon and Hance were piling the metal hooks with sharp, ringing echoes. All the others had vanished magically, at once, as if from an exhausted spell. Old Man Boeshore had departed with a piping implication, supported by Emanuel, his grandson.

Alexander Hulings was reviewing his material situation. It was three hundred and thirty dollars better than it had been on his arrival at Tubal Cain. In addition to that he had a new store of confidence, of indomitable pride, vanity, a more actual support. He gazed with interest toward the near future, and with no little doubt. It was patent that he could not proceed as he had begun; such combinations could not be forced a second time. He intended to remain at James Claypole's forge, conducting it as though it were his own—for the present, anyhow—but he should have to get an efficient working body; and many additions were necessary—among them a blacksmith shop. He had, with Conrad Wishon, the conviction that Clay-pole would not return.

More capital would be necessary. He was revolving this undeniable fact when, through the lush June foliage, he saw an open carriage turn from the road and descend to the forge clearing. It held an erect, trimly whiskered form and a negro driver. The former was John Wooddrop. He gazed with surprise, that increased to a recognition, a memory, of Alexander Hulings.

"Jim Claypole?" he queried.

"Not here," Hulings replied, even more laconically.

"Nonsense! I'm told he's been running Tubal Cain again. Say to him—and I've no time to dawdle—that John Wooddrop's here."

"Well, Claypole's not," the other repeated. "He's away. I'm running this forge—Alexander Hulings."

Wooddrop's mouth drew into a straight hard line from precise whisker to whisker. "I have been absent," he said finally. It was palpably an explanation, almost an excuse. Conrad Wishon appeared from within the forge shed. "Ah, Conrad!" John Wooddrop ejaculated pleasantly.

"Glad to find you at the hearth again. Come and see me in the morning."

"I think I'll stay here," the forgeman replied, "now Tubal Cain's working."

"Then, in a week or so," the Ironmaster answered imperturbably.

All Alexander Hulings' immaterial dislike of Wooddrop solidified into a concrete, vindictive enmity. He saw the beginning of a long, bitter, stirring struggle.

IV

THAT'. about it!" Conrad Wishon affirmed. They were seated by the doorway of the dwelling at Tubal Cain. It was night, and hot; and the heavy air was constantly fretted by distant, vague thunder. Alexander Hulings listened with pinched lips.

"I saw Derek, the founder at Blue Lump, and ordered the metal; then he told me that Wooddrop had sent word not to sell a pig outside his own forges. That comes near closing us up. I misdoubt that we could get men, anyhow—not without we went to Pittsburgh; and that would need big orders, big money. The old man's got us kind of shut in here, with only three mules and one wagon—we couldn't make out to haul any distance; and John Wooddrop picks up all the loose teams. It looks bad, that's what it does. No credit, too; I stopped at Harmony for some forge hooks, and they wouldn't let me take them away until you had paid. A word's been dropped there likewise." Hulings could see, without obvious statement, that his position was difficult; it was impossible seemingly, with his limited funds and equipment, to go forward and—no backward course existed: nothing but a void, ruin, the way across which had been destroyed. He turned with an involuntary dread from the fleeting contemplation of the past, mingled with monotony and suffering, and set all his cold, passionate mind on the problem of his future. He would, he told himself, succeed with iron here. He would succeed in spite of John Wooddrop—no, because of the Ironmaster; the latter increasingly served as an actual object of comparison, an incentive, and a deeply involved spectator.

He lost himself in a gratifying vision, when Conrad's voice, shattering the facile heights he had mounted, again fastened his attention on the exigencies of the present.

"A lot of money!" the other repeated. "I guess we'll have to shut down; but I'd almost rather drive mules on the canal that go to John Wood-drop."

Hulings declared: "You'll do neither, and Tubal Cain won't shut down!" He rose, turned into the house.

"What's up?" Wishon demanded at the sudden movement.

"I'm going after money," Hulings responded from within—"enough. A packet is due east before dawn."

If the canal boat had seemed to go slowly on his way to Harmony, it appeared scarcely to stir on his return. There was no immediate train connection at Columbus, and he footed the uneven shaded walks in an endless pattern, unconscious of houses, trees, or passing people, lost in the rehearsal of what he had to say, until the horn of an immediate departure summoned him to a seat in a coach.

The candles at each end sent a shifting, pale illumination over the cramped interior, voluminous skirts and prodigiously whiskered countenances. Each delay increased his impatience to a muttering fury; it irked him that he was unable to declare himself, Alexander Hulings, to the train captain, and by the sheer bulk of that name force a more rapid progress.

Finally in Eastlake, Veneada gazed at him out of a silent astonishment.

"You say you're Alex Hulings!" the doctor exclaimed. "Some of you seems to be; but the rest is—by heaven, iron! I'll admit now I was low about you when you left, in April; I knew you had gimp, and counted on it; however———"

The period expired in a wondering exhalation. Veneada pounded on his friend's chest, dug into his arm. "A horse!" he declared.

Alexander Hulings impatiently withdrew from the other's touch.

"Veneada," he said, "once you asked me to come to you if I wanted money, if I happened on a good thing. I said nothing at the time, because I couldn't picture an occasion when I'd do such a thing. Well—it's come. I need money, and I'm asking you for it. And, I warn you, it will be a big sum. If you can't manage it, I must go somewhere else; I'd go to China, if necessary—I'd stop people, strangers, on the street.

"A big sum," Hulings reiterated somberly; "perhaps ten, perhaps twenty, thousand. Not a loan," he added immediately, "but an investment—an investment in me. You must come out to Harmony. I can't explain: it wouldn't sound convincing in Eastlake. In the valleys, at Tubal Cain, the thing will be self-evident. I have made a beginning with practically nothing; and I can go on. But it will require capital, miles of forest, furnaces built, Pittsburgh swept bare of good men. No," he held up a hardened, arresting palm, "don't attempt to discuss it now. Come out to Tubal Cain and see; learn about John Wooddrop and how to turn iron into specie."

At the end of the week there were three chairs canted against the stone wall of the little house by the stream that drove Tubal Cain Forge. Conrad Wishon, with a scarlet undershirt open on a broad, hairy chest, listened with wonderment to the sharp periods of Alexander Hulings and Veneada; incredulously he heard mammoth sums of money estimated, projected, dismissed as commonplace. Veneada said:

"I've always believed in your ability, Alex; all that I questioned was the opportunity. Now that has gone; the chance is here. You've got those steel-wire fingers of yours about something rich, and you will never let go. It sounds absurd to go up against this Wooddrop, a despot and a firmly established power; anyone might well laugh at me, but I feel a little sorry for the older man. He doesn't know you.

"You haven't got insides, sympathies, weaknesses, like the others of us; the thing is missing in you that ordinarily betrays human men into slips; yes—compassion. You are not pretty to think about, Alex; but I suppose power never really is. You know I've got money and you know, too, that you can have it. As safe with you as in a bank vault!"

"We'll go back to Eastlake tomorrow," Hulings decided, "lay out our plans, and draw up papers. We'll buy the loose timber quietly through agents; I'll never appear in any of it. After that we can let out the contracts for two furnaces. I don't know anything about them now; but I shall in a week. Wishon had better live on here, pottering about the forge, until he can be sent to Pittsburgh after workmen. His pay will start tomorrow."

"What about Tubal Cain, and that fellow—what's his name?"

"Claypole, James. I'll keep a record of what his forge makes, along with mine, and bank it. Common safety. Then I must get over to New York, see the market there, men. I have had letters from an anchor foundry in Philadelphia. There are nail factories, locomotive shops, stove plate, to furnish. A hundred industries. I'll have them here in time—rolling mills you will hear back in the mountains. People on the packets will see the smoke of my furnaces—Alexander Hulings' iron!"

"You might furnish me with a pass, so that I could occasionally walk through and admire," Veneada said dryly.

Hulings never heard him.

"I'll have a mansion," he added abstractedly, "better than Wooddrop's, with more rooms——"

"All full, I suppose, of little glorious Hulingses!" the doctor interrupted.

Alexander regarded him unmoved. His thoughts suddenly returned to Hallie Flower. He saw her pale, strained face, her clasped hands; he heard the thin echo of her mingled patience and dismay: "Then I'll never be married!" There was no answering stir of regret, remorse; she slipped for ever out of his consciousness, as if she had been a shadow vanishing before a flood of hard, white light.

V

GREATLY to Alexander Hillings' relief, Doctor Veneada never considered the possibility of a partnership; it was as far from one man's wish, for totally different reasons, as from the other's.

"No, no, Alex," he declared; "I couldn't manage it. Some day, when you were out of the office, the widow or orphan would come in with the foreclosure, and I would tear up the papers. Seriously, I won't do—I'm fat and easy and lazy. My money would be safer with me carefully removed from the scene."

In the end Alexander protected Veneada with mortgages on the timber and land he secured about Harmony through various agents and under different names. Some of the properties he bought outright, but in the majority he merely purchased options on the timber. His holdings in the latter finally extended in a broad, irregular belt about the extended local industries of John Wooddrop. It would be impossible for the latter, when, in perhaps fifteen years, he had exhausted his present forests, to cut an acre of wood within practicable hauling distance. This accomplished, a momentary grim satisfaction was visible on Hulings' somber countenance.

He had, however, spent all the money furnished by Doctor Veneada, without setting the foundations of the furnaces and forges he had projected, and he decided not to go to his friend for more. There were two other possible sources of supply: allied iron industries—the obvious recourse—and the railroads. The latter seemed precarious; everywhere people, and even print, were ridiculing the final usefulness of steam traffic; it was judged unfit for heavy and continuous hauling—a toy of inventors and fantastic dreaming; canals were the obviously solid means of transportation. But Alexander Hulings became fanatical overnight in his belief in the coming empire of steam.

With a small carpetbag, holding his various deeds and options, and mentally formulating a vigorous expression of his opinions and projections, he sought the doubting capital behind the Columbus Transportation Line. When, a month later, he returned to Tubal Cain, it was in the company of an expert industrial engineer, and with credit sufficient for the completion of his present plans. He had been gone a month, but he appeared older by several years. Alexander Hulings had forced from reluctant sources, from men more wily, if less adamantine, than himself, what he desired; but in return he had been obliged to grant almost impossibly favorable contracts and preferences. A tremendous pressure of responsibility had gathered about him; but under it he was still erect, coldly confident, and carried himself with the special pugnacity of small, vain men.

On a day in early June, a year from the delivery of his first contract at Tubal Cain, he stood in a fine rain at the side of a light road wagon, drawn, like John Wooddrop's, by two sweeping young horses, held by a negro, and watched the final courses of his new furnace. The furnace itself, a solid structure of unmasoned stone, rose above thirty feet, narrowed at the top almost to half the width of its base. Directly against its face and hearth was built the single high interior of the cast house, into which the metal would be run on a sand pig bed to harden into commercial iron.

On the hill rising abruptly at the back was the long wall of the coal house, with an entrance and runway leading to the opening at the top of the furnace stack. Lower down, the curving artificial channel of the forebay swept to where the water would fall on a ponderous overshot wheel and drive the great tilted bellows that blasted the furnace.

The latter, Alexander knew, must have a name. Most furnaces were called after favorite women; but there were no such sentimental objects in his existence. He recalled the name of the canal packet that had first drawn him out to Harmony—the *Hit or Miss*. No casual title such as that would fit an enterprise of his. He thought of Tubal Cain, and then of Jim Claypole. He owed the latter something; and yet he wouldn't have another man's name.... Conrad Wishon had surmised that the owner of Tubal Cain had vanished—like Elijah—on a Glory-wagon. That was it—Glory Furnace! He turned and saw John Wooddrop leaning forward out of his equipage, keenly studying the new buildings.

"That's a good job," the Ironmaster allowed; "but it should be, built by Henry Bayard, the first man in the country. It ought to do very well for five or six years."

"Fifty," Hulings corrected him.

John Wooddrop's eyes were smiling.

"It's all a question of charcoal," he explained, as Wishon had, long before. "To be frank, I expect a little difficulty myself, later. It is surprising how generally properties have been newly bought in the county. I know, because lately I, too, have been reaching out. Practically all the available stuff has, been secured. Thousands of acres above you, here, have been taken by a company, hotel—or something of the sort."

"The Venealic Company," Hulings said; and then, in swelling pride, he added: "That's me!" Wooddrop's gaze hardened. Alexander Hulings thought the other's face grew paler. His importance, his sense of accomplishment, of vindication, completely overwhelmed him. "And beyond, it is me!" he cried. "And back of that, again!" He made a wide, sweeping gesture with his arm. "Over there; the Hezekiah Mills tract—that's me too; and the East purchase, and on and round. Fifty! This Glory Furnace, and ten others, could run on for a century.

"You've been the big thing here—even in the state. You are known on canal boats, people point you out; yes, and patronize me. You did that yourself—you and your women. But it is over; I'm coming now, and John Wooddrop's going. You are going with those same canal boats, and Alexander Hulings is rising with the railroads."

He pounded himself on the chest, and then suddenly stopped. It was the only impassioned speech, even in the disastrous pursuit of the law, that he had ever made; and it had an impotent, foolish ring in his ear, his deliberate brain. He instantly disowned all that part of him which had betrayed his ordinary silent caution into such windy boasting. Hulings was momentarily abashed before the steady scrutiny of John Wooddrop.

"When I first saw you," the latter pronounced, "I concluded that you were unbalanced. Now I think that you are a maniac!"

He spoke curtly to his driver, and was sharply whirled away through the grey-green veil of rain and foliage. Hulings was left with an aggravated discontent and bitterness toward the older man, who seemed to have the ability always to place him in an unfavorable light.

VI

DOCTOR VENEADA returned for the first run of metal from Glory Furnace; there were two representatives of the other capital invested, and, with Alexander Hulings, Conrad Wishon, and some local spectators, they stood in the gloom of the cast house waiting for the founder to tap the clay sealing of the hearth. Suddenly there was a rush of crackling white light, pouring sparks, and the boiling liquid flooded out, rapidly filling the molds radiating from the channels stamped in the sand bed. The incandescent iron flushed from silver to darker, warmer tones.

A corresponding warmth ran through Alexander Hulings' body; Glory Furnace was his; it had been conceived by him and his determination had brought it to an actuality. He would show Wood-drop a new type of "maniac." This was the second successful step in his move against the Ironmaster, in the latter's own field. Then he realized that he, too, might now be called Ironmaster. He directed extensive works operated under his name; he, Hulings, was the head! Already there were more than a hundred men to do what he directed, go where he wished. The feeling of power, of consequence, quickened through him. Alexander held himself, if possible, more rigidly than before; he followed every minute turn of the casting, tersely admonishing a laborer.

He was dressed with the utmost care; a marked niceness of apparel now distinguished him. His whiskers were closely trimmed, his hair brushed high under a glossy tile hat; he wore checked trousers, strapped on glazed Wellington boots, a broadcloth coat, fitted closely to his waist, with a deep rolling collar; severe neckcloth, and a number of seals on a stiff twill waistcoat. Veneada, as always, was carelessly garbed in wrinkled silk and a broad planter's hat. It seemed to Alexander that the other looked conspicuously older than he had only a few months back; the doctor's face was pendulous, the pouches beneath his eyes livid.

Alexander Hulings quickly forgot this in the immediate pressure of manufacture. The younger Wishon, who had followed his father into Alexander's service, now came down from the charcoal stacks in a great sectional wagon drawn by six mules, collared in bells and red streamers. The pigs were sledged in endless procession from Glory, and then from a second furnace, to the forges that reached along the creek in each direction from Tubal Cain. The latter was worked as vigorously as possible, but Alexander conducted its finances in a separate, private column; all the profit he banked to the credit of James Claypole. He did this not from a sense of equity, but because of a deeper, more obscure feeling, almost a superstition, that such acknowledgment of the absent man's unwitting assistance was a safeguard of further good fortune.

The months fled with amazing rapidity; it seemed to him that one day the ground was shrouded in snow, and on the next the dogwood was blooming. No man in all his properties worked harder or through longer hours than Alexander; the night shift at a forge would often see him standing grimly in the lurid reflections of the hearths; charcoal burners, eating their flitch and potatoes on an outlying mountain, not infrequently heard the beat of his horse's hoofs on the soft moss, his domineering voice bullying them for some slight oversight. He inspired everywhere a dread mingled with grudging admiration; it was known that he forced every possible ounce of effort from workman and beast.

Nevertheless, toward the end of the third summer of his success he contracted a lingering fever, and he was positively commanded to leave his labors for a rest and change. Wrapped in a shawl, he sat on the porch of the house he had commenced building, on a rise overlooking the eddying smoke of his industries, and considered the various places that offered relaxation; he could go to the sea, at Long Branch, or to Saratoga, the gayety and prodigality of which were famous.... But his thought returned to his collapse four years before; he heard Veneada counseling him to take the water of the Mineral Springs. He had been too poor then for the Mineral; had he gone there, he would have arrived unnoticed. By heaven, he would go there now! It was, he knew, less fashionable than the other places; its day had been twenty, thirty years before. But it represented once more his progress, his success; and, in the company of his personal servant, his leather boxes strapped at the back of his lightest road wagon, he set out the following morning.

Almost sixty miles of indifferent roads lay before him; and, though he covered, in his weakened condition, far more than half the distance by evening, he was forced to stay overnight at a roadside tavern. The way was wild and led through narrow, dark valleys, under the shadow of uninhabited ridges, and through swift fords. Occasionally he passed great, slow Conestoga wagons, entrained for the West; leather-hooded, ancient vehicles; and men on horses.

The wagon broke suddenly info the smooth, green valley that held the Mineral Springs. Against a western mountain were grouped hotels; a bridge, crossing a limpid stream; pointed kiosks in the Chinese taste; and red gravel walks. The hotel before which Alexander stopped—a prodigiously long, high structure painted white—had a deep porch across its face with slender columns towering up unbroken to the roof and festooned with trumpet flowers. A bell rang loudly for dinner; and there was a colorful flow of crinoline over the porch, a perfumed flowery stir, through which he impatiently made his way, followed by negro boys with his luggage.

Within, the office was high and bare, with a sweeping staircase, and wide doors opened on a lofty thronged dining room. Above, he was led through interminable narrow corridors, past multitudinous closed doors, to a closetlike room completely filled by a narrow bed, a chair, and a corner washstand; this, with some pegs in the calcined wall and a bell rope, completed the provisions for his comfort. His toilet was hurried, for he had been warned that extreme promptness at meals was more than desirable; and, again below, he was led by a pompous negro between long, crowded tables to a place at the farther end. The din of conversation and clatter of dishes were deafening. In the ceiling great connected fans were languidly pulled by black boys, making a doubtful circulation.

His dinner was cold and absurdly inadequate, but the table claret was palatable. And, after the isolation of Tubal Cain, the droves of festive people absorbed him. Later, at the bar, he came across an acquaintance, a railroad director, who pointed out to Alexander what notables were present. There was an Englishman, a lord; there was Bartram Ainscough, a famous gambler; there— Alexander's arm was grasped by his companion.

"See that man—no, farther—dark, in a linen suit? Well, that's Partridge Sinnox, of New Orleans." He grew slightly impatient at Hulings' look of inquiry. "Never heard of him! Best-known pistol shot in the States. A man of the highest honor. Will go out on the slightest provocation." His voice lowered. "He's said to have killed twelve—no less. His companion there, from Louisiana too, never leaves him. Prodigiously rich: canefields."

Alexander Hulings looked with small interest at the dueller and his associate. The former had a lean, tanned face, small black eyes that held each a single point of light, and long, precise hands. Here, Alexander thought, was another form of publicity, different from his own. As always, his lips tightened in a faint contempt at pretensions other than his, or threatening to his preëminence. Sinnox inspired none of the dread or curiosity evident in his companion; and he turned from him to the inspection of a Pennsylvania coal magnate.

The colonnade of the hotel faced another cultivated ridge, on which terraced walks mounted to a pavilion at the crest; and there, through the late afternoon, he rested and gazed down at the Springs or over to the village beyond. Alexander was wearier than he had supposed; the iron seemed suddenly insupportably burdensome; a longing for lighter, gayer contacts possessed him. He wanted to enter the relaxations of the Springs.

Dancing, he knew, was customary after supper; and he lingered over a careful toilet—bright blue coat, tight black trousers, and flat, glistening slippers, with a soft cambric ruffle. Alexander Hulings surveyed his countenance in a scrap of mirror, and saw, with mingled surprise and discontent, that he—like

Veneada—bore unmistakable signs of age, marks of strife and suffering; his whiskers had an evident silvery sheen. Life, receding unnoticed, had set him at the verge of middle age. But at least, he thought, his was not an impotent medial period; if, without material success, he had unexpectedly seen the slightly drawn countenance meeting him in the mirror, he would have killed himself. He realized that coldly. He could never have survived an established nonentity. As it was, descending the stairs to supper, immaculate and disdainful, he was upheld by the memory of his accomplishments, his widening importance, weight. He actually heard a whispered comment: "Hulings, iron."

VII

AFTER supper the furnishings of the dining room were swept aside by a troop of waiters, while a number of the latter, with fiddles and comets, were grouped on a table, over which a green doth had been spread. With the inevitable scraping of strings and preliminary unattended dance, a quadrille was formed. Alexander, lounging with other exactly garbed males in the doorway, watched with secret envy the participants in the figures gliding from one to another. As if from another life he recalled their names; they were dancing Le Pantalon now; La Poulee would follow; then the Pastorale and L'.té.

Above the spreading gauze, the tulle and glacé silks of the women, immense candelabra of glass pendants and candles shone and glittered; the rustle of crinoline, of light passing feet, sounded below the violins and blown comets, the rich husky voices calling the changes of the quadrille.

He was troubled by an obscure desire to be a center of interest, of importance, for the graceful feminine world about him. Sinnox, the man from New Orleans, was bowing profoundly to his partner; a figure broke up into a general boisterous gallopading—girls, with flushed cheeks, swinging curls, spun from masculine shoulder to shoulder. The dance ended, and the floating, perfumed skirts passed him in a soft flood toward the porch.

Without, the colonnade towered against a sky bright with stars; the night was warm and still. Alexander Hulings was lonely; he attempted to detain the acquaintance met in the bar, but the other, bearing a great bouquet of rosebuds in a lace-paper cone, hurried importantly away. A subdued barytone was singing: "Our Way Across the Mountain, Ho!" The strains of a waltz, the Carlotta-Grisi, drifted out, and a number of couples answered its invitation.

A group at the iron railing across the foot of the colonnade attracted his attention by its excessive gayety. The center, he saw, was a young woman, with smooth bandeaux and loops of black hair, and a goya lily caught below her ear. She was not handsome, but her features were animated, and her shoulders as finely white and sloping as an alabaster vase.

It was not this that held his attention, but a sense of familiarity, a feeling that he had seen her before. He walked past the group, without plan, and, meeting her gaze, bowed awkwardly in response to a hesitating but unmistakable smile of recognition. Alexander stopped, and she imperiously waved him to join the number about her. He was in a cold dread of the necessity of admitting, before so many, that he could not recall her name; but obviously all that she desired was to swell the circle of her admirers, for, beyond a second nod, she ignored him.

The Southerner was at her shoulder, maintaining a steady flow of repartee, and Alexander envied him his assured presence, his dark, distinguished appearance. The man who had been indicated as Sinnox' companion stood by Hulings, and the latter conceived a violent prejudice for the other's meager yellow face and spiderlike hand, employed with a cheroot.

Alexander hoped that somebody would repeat the name of the girl who had spoken to him. A woman did, but only in the contracted, familiar form of Gisela.... Gisela—he had heard that too. Suddenly she affected to be annoyed; she arched her fine brows and glanced about, her gaze falling upon Alexander Hulings. Before he was aware of her movement a smooth white arm was thrust through his; he saw the curve of a powdered cheek, an elevated chin.

"Do take me out of this!" she demanded. "New Orleans molasses is—well, too thick."

Obeying the gentle pressure of her arm, he led her down the steps to the graveled expanse below. She stopped by a figure of the Goddess of Health, in filigree on mossy rocks, pouring water from an urn. Her gown was glazed green muslin, with a mist of white tulle, shining with particles of silver. The goya lily exhaled a poignant scent.

"I didn't really leave because of Mr. Sinnox," she admitted; "a pin was scratching, and I was devoured with curiosity to know who you were, where I had met——"

Suddenly, in a flash of remembered misery, of bitter resentment, he recognized her—Gisela, John Wooddrop's daughter. The knowledge pinched at his heart with malicious fingers; the starry night, the music and gala attire, his loneliness had betrayed him into an unusual plasticity of being. He delayed for a long breath, and then said dryly: "I'm Alexander Hullings."

"Not——" she half cried, startled. She drew away from him, and her face grew cold. In the silence that followed he was conscious of the flower's perfume and the insistent drip of the water falling from the urn. "But I haven't met you at all," she said; "I don't in the least know you." Her attitude was insolent, and yet she unconsciously betrayed a faint curiosity. "I think you lacked delicacy to join my friends—to bring me out here!"

"I didn't," he reminded her; "you brought me." Instantly he cursed such clumsy stupidity. Her lower lip protruded disdainfully.

"Forgive me," she said, dropping a curtsy, "but I needn't keep you."

She swept away across the gravel and up the stairs to the veranda. It was evident that the group had not separated; for almost immediately there rose a concerted laughter, a palpable mockery, drifting out to Alexander.

His face was hot, his hands clenched in angry resentment. More than anything else, he shrank from being an object of amusement, of gibes. It was necessary to his self-esteem to be met with grave appreciation.

This was his first experience of the keen assaults of social weapons, and it inflicted on him an extravagant suffering. His instinct was to retire farther into the night, only to return to his room when the hotel was dark, deserted. But a second, stronger impulse sent him deliberately after Gisela Wooddrop, up the veranda stairs, and rigidly past the group gazing at him with curious mirth.

An oil flare fixed above them shone down on the lean, saturnine countenance of Partridge Sinnox. The latter, as he caught Alexander Hulings' gaze, smiled slightly.

That expression followed Alexander to his cramped room; it mocked him as he viciously pulled at the bell rope, desiring his servant; it was borne up to him on the faint strains of the violins. And in the morning it clouded his entire outlook. Sinnox' smile expressed a contempt that Alexander Hulings' spirit could not endure. From the first he had been resentful of the Southerner's cheap prestige. He added the qualifying word as he descended to breakfast.

Sinnox, as a dueller, roused Hulings' impatience; he had more than once faced impromptu death—iron bars in the hands of infuriated employees, and he had overborne them with a cold phrase. This theatrical playing with pistols—cheap! Later, in the crowded bar, he was pressed elbow to elbow with Sinnox and his companion; and he automatically and ruthlessly cleared sufficient space for his comfort. Sinnox' associate said, in remonstrance: "Sir, there are others—perhaps more considerable."

"Perhaps!" Alexander Hulings carelessly agreed. Sinnox gazed down on him with narrowed eyes. "I see none about us," he remarked, "who would have to admit the qualification."

Alexander's bitterness increased, became aggressive. He met Sinnox' gaze with a stiff, dangerous scorn:

"In your case, at least, it needn't stand."

"Gentlemen," the third cried, "no more, I beg of you." He grasped Alexander Hulings' arm. "Withdraw!" he advised. "Mr. Sinnox' temper is fatal. Beyond a certain point it cannot be leashed. It has caused great grief. Gentlemen, I beg——"

"Do you mean——" Sinnox demanded, and his face was covered by an even, dark flush to the sweep of his hair.

"Cheap!" Alexander's voice was sudden and unpremeditated.

The other's temper rose in a black passion; he became so enraged that his words were mere unintelligible gasps. His hand shook so that he dropped a glass of rock-and-rye splintering on the floor. "At once!" he finally articulated. "Scurvy——"

"This couldn't be helped," his companion proclaimed, agitated. "I warned the other gentleman. Mr. Sinnox is not himself in a rage, his record is well known. He was elbowed aside by——"

"Alexander Hulings!" that individual pronounced.

He was aware of the gaze of the crowding men about him; already he was conscious of an admiration roused by the mere fact of his facing a notorious bully. Cheap! The director joined him.

"By heavens, Hulings, you're in dangerous water. I understand you have no family."

"None!" Alexander stated curtly.

Illogically he was conscious of the scent of a goya lily. Sinnox was propelled from the bar, and his friend reappeared and conferred with the director.

"At once!" Hulings heard the former announce. "Mr. Sinnox... unbearable!"

"Have you a case of pistols?" the director asked. "Mr. Sinnox offers his. I believe there is a quiet opening back of the bathhouse. But my earnest advice to you is to withdraw; you will be very little blamed; this man is notorious, a professional fighter. You have only to say——"

Cheap! Alexander thought again, fretful at having been involved in such a ridiculous affair. He was even more deliberate than usual; but, though he was certain of his entire normality, the faces about him resembled small, bobbing balloons.

Alexander finished his drink—surprised to find himself still standing by the bar—and silently followed the director through the great hall of the hotel out on to the veranda, and across the grass to a spot hidden from the valley by the long, low bulk of the bathing house.

Sinnox and his companion, with a polished mahogany box, were already there; a small, curious group congregated in the distance. Sinnox' friend produced long pistols with silken-brown barrels and elegantly carved ivory stocks, into which he formally rammed powder and balls. Alexander Hulings was composed; but his fingers were cold, slightly numb, and he rubbed them together angrily. Not for an instant did he think that he might be killed; other curious, faint emotions assailed him—long-forgotten memories of distant years; Veneada's kindly hand on his shoulder; the mule called Alexander because of its aptitude for hard labor; John Wooddrop's daughter.

He saw that the pistols had been loaded; their manipulator stood with them, butts extended, in his grasp. He began a preamble of customary explanation, which he ended by demanding, for his principal, an apology from Alexander Hulings. The latter, making no reply, was attracted by Sin-nox' expression of deepening passion; the man's face, he thought, positively was black. Partridge Sinnox' entire body was twitching with rage.... Curious, for a seasoned, famous dueller!

Suddenly Sinnox, with a broken exclamation, swung on his heel, grasped one of the pistols in his second's hands, and discharged it point-blank at Alexander Hulings.

An instant confused outcry rose. Alexander heard the term "Insane!" pronounced, as if in extenuation, by Sinnox' friend. The latter held the remaining, undischarged pistol out of reach; the other lay on the ground before Partridge Sinnox. Alexander's face was as grey as granite.

"That was the way he did it," he unconsciously pronounced aloud.

He wondered slowly at the fact that he had been unhit. Then, with his hand in a pocket, he walked stiffly up to within a few feet of Sinnox, and produced a small, ugly derringer, with one blunt barrel on top of the other.

At the stunning report that followed, the vicious, stinging cloud of smoke, he seemed to wake. He felt himself propelled away from the vicinity of the bathhouse; low, excited exclamations beat upon his ears: "Absolutely justified!"

"Horrible attempt to murder!"

"Get his nigger and things. Best for the present." He impatiently shook himself free from his small following.

"Did I kill him?" he demanded.

There was an affirmative silence.

In his wagon, driving rapidly toward Tubal Cain, a sudden sense of horror, weakness, overtook him; the roadside rocked beneath his vision.

"Mordecai," he said to his coachman, "I—I shot a man, derringered him."

The negro was unmoved.

"Man 'at fool round you, he's bound to be killed!" he asserted. "Yes, sir; he just throwed himself right away!"

Alexander Hulings wondered how John Wood-drop's daughter would be affected. At least, he thought grimly, once more self-possessed, he had put a stop to her laughter at his expense.

VIII

IN the weeks that followed he devoted himself energetically to the finishing of the mansion in course of erection above Tubal Cain. It was an uncompromising, square edifice of brick, with a railed belvedere on the roof, and a front lawn enclosed by a cast-iron fence. On each side of the path dividing the sod were wooden Chinese pagodas like those he had seen at the Mineral Springs; masoned rings for flower beds, and ferneries, artificially heaped stones, with a fine spray from concealed pipes. Rearing its solid bulk against the living greenery of the forest, it was, he told himself pridefully, a considerable dwelling. Within were high walls and flowery ceilings, Italian marble mantels and tall mirrors, black carved and gilded furniture, and brilliant hassocks on thick-piled carpet.

The greater part of the labor was performed by the many skilled workmen now employed in his furnaces and forges. He was utterly regardless of cost, obligations; of money itself. Alexander had always been impatient at the mere material fact of wealth, of the possession and the accumulation of sheer gold. To him it was nothing more than a lever by which he moved men and things; it was a ladder that carried him above the unnoticed and unnotable. He could always get money, at need, from men or iron; to debts he never gave a thought—when they fell due they were discharged or carried forward.

His reason for finishing his dwelling with such elaboration was obscure. Veneada had laughed at him, speaking of small Hulingses, but he harbored no concrete purpose of marriage; there was even no dominant feminine figure in his thoughts. Perhaps faintly at times he caught the odor of a goya lily; but that was probably due to the fact that lilies were already blooming in the circular conservatory of highly colored glass attached to his veranda.

The greater part of the house was darkened, shrouded in linen. He would see, when walking through the hall, mysterious and shadowy vistas, lengthened endlessly in the long mirrors, of dusky carpet and alabaster and ormolu, the faint glitter of the prisms hung on the mantel lamps. Clocks would strike sonorously in the depths of halls, with the ripple of cathedral chimes. He had a housekeeper, a stout person in oiled curls, and a number of excessively humble negro servants. Alexander Hulings got from all this an acute pleasure. It, too, was a mark of his success.

He had, below, on the public road, a small edifice of one room, which formed his office, and there he saw the vast number of men always consulting with him; he never took them above to his house. And when they dined with him it was at the hotel, newly built by the packet station on the canal—functions flooded with the prodigal amounts of champagne Hulings thought necessary to his importance.

Most of his days were spent in his road wagon, in which he traveled to Pittsburgh, West Virginia, Philadelphia, where he had properties or interests. In the cities of his associates he also avoided their homes, and met them in hotels, discussed the terms of business in bars or public parlors. With women of position he was at once indifferent and ill at ease, constantly certain that he was not appearing to good advantage, and suspecting their asides and enigmatic smiles. He was laboriously, stiffly polite, speaking in complimentary flourishes that sometimes ended in abrupt constraint. At this, afterward, he would chafe, and damn the superior airs of women.

He had returned from such an expedition to Wheeling, and was sitting in his office, when a vehicle pulled up before his door. Deliberate feet approached, and John Wooddrop entered. The latter, Alexander realized enviously, was an excessively handsome old man; he had a commanding height and a square, highly colored countenance, with dose white sideburns and vigorous silver hair. His manner, too, was assured and easy. He greeted Alexander Hulings with a keen, open smile.

"Everything is splendid here!" he proclaimed. "I looked in that chafery down stream, and the metal was worked like satin. Fine weather for the furnaces—rain's ugly; a furnace is like a young girl."

Hulings wondered—contained and suspicious—what the other wanted. Wooddrop, though they passed each other frequently on the road, had not saluted him since the completion of Glory Furnace. He thought for a moment that already the older man was feeling the pinch of fuel scarcity and that he had come to beg for timber. In such a case Alexander Hulings decided coldly that he would not sell Wooddrop an ell of forest. In addition to the fact that the complete success of one or the other depended ultimately on his rival's failure, he maintained a personal dislike of John Wooddrop; he had never forgotten the humiliation forced on him long before, in the dining room of the packet, the *Hit or Miss*; he could not forgive Wooddrop's preeminence in the iron field. The latter was a legend of the manufacture of iron.

However, any idea of the other's begging privilege was immediately banished by John Wood-drop's equable bearing. He said:

"I want to speak to you, Hulings, about a rather delicate matter. In a way it is connected with my daughter, Gisela. You saw her, I believe, at the Springs."

Alexander Hulings somberly inclined his head.

"Of course," Wooddrop continued, "I heard about the difficulty you had with that Louisiana bravo. I understand you acted like a man of spirit and were completely exonerated; in fact, I had some small part in quashing legal complications. This was done not on your account, but because of Gisela, who confided to me that she held herself in blame. Mr. Hulings," he said gravely, "my feeling for my daughter is not the usual affection of parent for child. My wife is dead. Gisela—— But I won't open a personal subject with you. I spoke as I did merely, in a way, to prepare you for what follows. My daughter felt that she did you a painful wrong; and I have come, in consequence, to offer you my good will. I propose that we end our competition and proceed together, for the good of both. Consolidated, we should inevitably control the iron situation in our state; you are younger, more vigorous than myself, and I have a certain prestige. Sir, I offer you the hand of friendly cooperation."

Alexander Hulings' gaze narrowed as he studied the man before him. At first, he had searched for an ulterior motive, need, in Wooddrop's proposal; but he quickly saw that the proposal had been completely stated. Illogically he thought of black ringleted hair and glazed muslin; he heard the echo of water dripping from a stone urn. Lost in memories, he was silent, for so long that John Wood-drop palpably grew impatient. He cleared his throat sharply; but Hulings didn't shift a muscle. Alexander was thinking now of the order he had filled the first summer at Tubal Cain, of his brutal labor and bitter, deferred aspirations. His rise, alone, had been at the price of ceaseless struggle; it was not yet consummated; but it would be—it must, and still alone. Nothing should rob him of the credit of his accomplishment; no person coupled with him might reduce or share his triumph. What he said sounded inexcusably harsh after the other's open manner.

"Only," he said, "only if the amalgamated industries bear my name—the Alexander Hulings Ironworks."

John Wooddrop's face darkened as he comprehended the implied insult to his dignity and position. He rose, so violently thrusting back the chair in which he had been sitting, that it fell with a clatter.

"You brass trumpet!" he ejaculated. "You intolerable little bag of vanity! Will you never see yourself except in a glass of flattery or intolerable self-satisfaction? It would be impossible to say which you inspire most, contempt or pity."

Strangely enough, Hulings didn't resent the language applied to him. He gazed at Wooddrop without anger. The other's noise, he thought, was but a symptom of his coming downfall. He was slowly but surely drawing the rope about the throat of Wooddrop's industries.

"Absolutely the last time," the other stuttered. "Now you can go to hell on your own high horse! Blinded by your own fatuousness—don't see where the country is running. You may impose on others, but I know your business, sir; and it's as hollow as a tin plate stove. The times will soon kick it in."

John Wooddrop stamped away from Hillings in a rage.

IX

THAT evening Alexander Hulings wondered what Gisela had told her father; he won-ered more vaguely what she had thought of him—what, if at all, she still thought. He had had a formal room illuminated for his cigar after dinner; and he sat, a small, precise figure, with dust-colored hair and a somber, intent countenance, clasping a heavy roll of expensive tobacco, in a crimson plush chair. The silence, the emptiness about him was filled with rich color, ponderous maroon draperies, marble slabs and fretted tulip-wood.

It suddenly struck him that, by himself, he was slightly ridiculous in such opulence. His house needed a mistress, a creature of elegance to preside at his table, to exhibit in her silks and jewels another sign of his importance. Again, as if from the conservatory, he caught a faint poignant perfume.

Gisela Wooddrop was a person of distinction, self-possessed and charming. There was a subtle flavor in thus considering her father's daughter—old Wooddrop's girl—and himself. He rose and walked to a mirror, critically surveying his countenance; yes, it was well marked by age, yet it was sharp in outline; his step was springy; he felt none of the lassitude of increasing years.

He was in his prime. Many young women would prefer him, his house and name, to the windy pretensions of youthful scapegoats. A diamond necklace was a convincing form of courtship. There was no absolute plan in his thoughts that night; but, in the dry romantic absorption of the days that followed, a fantastic purpose formed and increased—he determined to marry Gisela Wood-drop.

He had for this, he assured himself, some slight encouragement; it was patent that her father had entirely misread the girl's intent in suggesting an end to the hostilities which had made impossible any social intercourse. She was interested in him; the duel with Sinnox had captured her imagination. Women responded surprisingly to such things. Then she had held that it had been partly her fault! Now it seemed to him that he understood why he had built so elaborately since his return from the Mineral Springs; unconsciously—all the while—it had been for his wife, for Gisela.

There were great practical difficulties in the realization of his desire, even in his opportunity to present his question; to see Gisela Wooddrop long enough and sufficiently privately to explain all he hoped. He was, too, far past the age of romantic assignations, episodes; he could no more decorate a moonlit scene beneath a window. Alexander must not count on adventitious assistance from emotional setting: his offer could carry only its grave material solidity. Often he laughed curtly at what momentarily seemed an absurd fantasy, a madness approaching senility; then his pride would flood back, reassert the strength of his determination, the desirability of Alexander Hulings.

X

THE occasion evaded him; the simplicity of his wish, of the bald relationship between the Wooddrops and Tubal Cain, preventing it more surely than a multiplication of barriers. He never considered the possibility of a compromise with John Wooddrop, a retreat from his position. Alexander thought of Gisela as a possible addition to his dignity and standing—of the few women he had seen she possessed the greatest attractions—and he gave no thought of a sacrifice to gain her. She was to be a piece with the rest of his success—a wife to honor his mansion, to greet a selected few of his friends, and wear the gold and jewels purchased by the Hulings iron.

He made no overt attempt to see her, but waited for opportunity. Meantime he had commenced to think of her in terms of passionless intimacy. Alexander Hulings was a solitary man; except for his industrial activity his mind was empty; and Gisela Wooddrop quickly usurped the hours after dinner, the long drives through massed and unscarred forests. He recalled her minutely—every expression that he had seen, every variation of dress. Wooddrop's daughter was handsomely provided for; but Alexander Hulings' wife would be a revelation in luxury. In New York he bought a pair of India cashmere shawls, paying a thousand dollars for them, and placed them on a chair, ready.

The weeks multiplied; and he got such pleasure from the mere thought of Gisela sweeping through his rooms, accompanying him to Philadelphia, shining beside him at the opera, that he became almost reluctant to force the issue of her choice. He was more than customarily careful with his clothes; his silk hats were immaculate; his trousers ranged in color from the most delicate sulphur to astounding London checks; he had his yellow boots polished with champagne, his handkerchiefs scented with essence of nolette and almond. For all this, his countenance was none the less severe, his aptitude for labor untouched; he followed every detail of iron manufacture, every improved process, every shift in the market.

The valley about Tubal Cain now resembled a small, widely scattered town; the dwellings of Hulings' workmen extended to the property line of the Blue Lump Furnace; roads were cut, bridges thrown across the stream. The flutter of wings, the pouring birdsong and vale of green, that Alexander had found had given place to a continuous, shattering uproar day and night; the charging of furnaces, the dull thunder of the heavy wagons of blooms, the jangle of shingling sledges and monotonous fall of trip hammers, mingled and rose in a stridulous volume to the sky, accompanied by chemical vapors, uprushing cinders and the sooty smoke of the forges. A company store had been built and stocked, and grimy troops of laborers were perpetually gathered, off shift, by its face.

Harmony itself, the station on the canal, had expanded; the new hotel, an edifice of brick with a steep slate roof and iron grilling, faced a rival saloon and various emporia of merchandise. An additional basin had been cut in the bank for the loading of Alexander Hulings' iron on to the canal boats.

He had driven to the canal—it was early summer—to see about a congestion of movement; and, hot, he stopped in the hotel for a pint of wine in a high glass with cracked ice. The lower floor was cut in half by a hall and stairs; on the right the bar opened on the narrow porch, while at the left a ladies' entrance gave way to the inevitable dark, already musty parlor. The bar was crowded, and, intolerant of the least curtailment of his dignity or comfort, he secured his glass and moved across the hall to the stillness of the parlor.

A woman was standing, blurred in outline, at one of the narrow windows. She turned as he entered; he bowed, prepared to withdraw, when he saw that it was Gisela Wooddrop. She wore white muslin, sprigged in orange chenille, with green ribbons, and carried a green parasol. Alexander stood motionless in the doorway, his champagne in one hand and a glossy stovepipe hat in the other. He was aware of a slight inward confusion, but outwardly he was unmoved, exact. Gisela, too, maintained the turn of her flexible body, her hands on the top of the parasol. Under her bonnet her face was pale, her eyes noticeably bright. Alexander Hulings said:

"Good afternoon!"

He moved into the room. Gisela said nothing; she was like a graceful painted figure on a shadowy background. A complete ease possessed Alexander.

"Miss Wooddrop," he continued, in the vein of a simple statement. She nodded automatically. "This is a happy meeting—for me. I can now express my gratitude for your concern about a certain unfortunate occurrence at the Mineral Springs. At the same time, I regret that you were caused the slightest uneasiness."

She shuddered delicately.

"Nothing more need be said about that," she told him. "I explained to my father; but I was sorry afterward that I did it, and—and put him to fresh humiliation."

"There," he gravely replied, "little enough can be discussed. It has to do with things that you would have limited patience with, strictly an affair of business. I was referring to your susceptibility of heart, a charming female quality."

He bowed stiffly. Gisela came nearer to him, a sudden emotion trembling on her features.

"Why don't you end it?" she cried, low and distressed. "It has gone on a long while now—the bitterness between you; I am certain in his heart father is weary of it, and you are younger——"

She broke off before the tightening of his lips. "Not a topic to be developed here," he insisted. He had no intention, Alexander Hulings thought, of being bent about even so charming a finger. And it was well to establish at once the manner in which any future they might share should be conducted. He wanted a wife, not an intrigante nor Amazon. Her feeling, color, rapidly evaporated, and left her pallid, confused, before his calm demeanor. She turned her head away, her face lost in the bonnet, but slowly her gaze returned to meet his keen inquiry. His impulse was to ask her, then, at once, to marry him; but he restrained that headlong course, feeling that it would startle her into flight. As it was, she moved slowly toward the door.

"I am to meet a friend on the Western packet," she explained; "I thought I heard the horn."

"It was only freight," he replied. "I should be sorry to lose this short opportunity to pay you my respects; to tell you that you have been a lot in my thoughts lately. I envy the men who see you casually, whenever they choose."

She gazed at him with palpable surprise gathering in her widely opened eyes. "But," she said breathlessly, "everybody knows that you never address a polite syllable to a woman. It is more speculated on than any of your other traits."

He expanded at this indication of a widespread discussion of his qualities.

"I have had no time for merely polite speeches," he responded. "And I assure you that I am not only complimentary now; I mean that I am not saluting you with vapid elegance. I am awaiting only a more fitting occasion to speak further."

She circled him slowly, with a minute whispering of crinoline, her gaze never leaving his face. Her muslin, below her white, bare throat, circled by a black velvet band, was heaving. The parasol fell with a clatter. He stooped immediately; but she was before him and snatched it up, with crimson cheeks.

"They say that you are the most hateful man alive!" she half breathed.

"Who are 'they'." he demanded contemptuously. "Men I have beaten and women I failed to see. That hatred grows with success, with power; it is never wasted on the weak. My competitors would like to see me fall into a furnace stack—the men I have climbed over, and my debtors. They are combining every month to push me to the wall, a dozen of them together, yelping like a pack of dogs. But they haven't succeeded; they never will!" His words were like the chips from an iron bloom. "They never will," he repeated harshly, "and I have only begun. I want you to see my house sometime. I planned a great part of it with you in mind. No money was spared.... I should be happy to have you like it. I think of it as yours."

All the time he was speaking she was stealing by imperceptible degrees toward the door; but at his last, surprising sentence she stood transfixed with mingled wonder and fear. She felt behind her for the open doorway and rested one hand against the woodwork. A ribald clatter sounded from the bar, and without rose the faint, clear note of an approaching packet. Her lips formed for speech, but only a slight gasp was audible; then her spreading skirts billowed through the opening, and she was gone.

Alexander Hulings found that he was still holding his silk hat; he placed it carefully on the table and took a deep drink from the iced glass. He was conscious of a greater feeling of triumph than he had ever known before. He realized that he had hardly needed to add the spoken word to the impression his being had made on Gisela Wood-drop. He had already invaded her imagination; the legend of his struggle and growth had taken possession of her. There remained now only a formal declaration, the outcome of which he felt almost certain would be in his favor.

Again in his house, he inspected the silk hangings of the particularly feminine chambers. He trod the thick carpets with a keen anticipation of her exclamations of pleasure, her surprise at convenient trifle after trifle. In the stable he surveyed a blooded mare she might take a fancy to; he must buy a light carriage, with a fringed canopy—yes, and put a driver into livery. Women liked such things.

At dinner he speculated on the feminine palate; he liked lean mountain venison, and a sherry that left almost a sensation of dust on the tongue; but women preferred sparkling hock and pastry, fruit preserved in white brandy, and pagodas of barley sugar.

Through the open windows came the subdued clatter of his forges; the hooded candles on the table flickered slightly in a warm eddy, while corresponding shadows stirred on the heavy napery, the Sheffield, and delicate creamy Belleek of his dinner service—the emblem of his certitude and pride.

XI

IN October Alexander Hulings took Gisela Wooddrop to the home that had been so largely planned for her enjoyment. They had been married in a private parlor of the United States Hotel, in Philadelphia; and after a small supper had gone to the Opera House to see "Love in a Village," followed by a musical *pasticcio*. Gisela's mother had died the winter before, and she was attended by an elderly distant cousin; no one else was present at the wedding ceremony except a friend of Gisela's—a girl who wept copiously—and Doctor Veneada. The latter's skin hung in loose folds, like a sack partially emptied of its contents; his customary spirit had evaporated too; and he sat through the wedding supper neither eating nor speaking, save for the forced proposal of the bride's health.

Gisela Wooddrop and Alexander Hulings, meeting on a number of carefully planned, apparently accidental occasions, had decided to be married while John Wooddrop was confined to his room by severe gout. In this manner they avoided the unpleasant certainty of his refusal to attend his daughter's, and only child's, wedding. Gisela had not told Alexander Hulings what the aging Ironmaster had said when necessarily informed of her purpose. No message had come to Alexander from John Wooddrop; since the ceremony the Hulingses had had no sign of the other's existence.

Alexander surveyed his wife with huge satisfaction as they sat for the first time at supper in their house. She wore white, with the diamonds he had given her about her firm young throat, black-enamel bracelets on her wrists, and her hair in a gilt net. She sighed with deep pleasure.

"It's wonderful!" she proclaimed, and then corroborated all he had surmised about the growth of her interest in him; it had reached forward and back from the killing of Partridge Sinnox. "That was the first time," she told him, "that I realized you were so—so big. You looked so miserable on the canal boat, coming out here those years ago, that it hardly seemed possible for you merely to live; and when you started the hearths at Tubal Cain everyone who knew anything about iron just laughed at you—we used to go down sometimes and look at those killing workmen you had, and that single mule and old horse.

"I wasn't interested then, and I don't know when it happened; but now I can see that a time soon came when men stopped laughing at you. I can just remember when father first became seriously annoyed, when he declared that he was going to force you out of the valleys at once. But it seemed you didn't go. And then in a few months he came home in a dreadful temper, when he found that you controlled all the timber on the mountains. He said of course you would break before he was really short of charcoal. But it seems you haven't broken. And now I'm married to you; I'm Gisela Hulings!"

"This is hardly more than the beginning," he added; "the foundation—just as iron is the base for so much. I—we—are going on," he corrected the period lamely, but was rewarded by a charming smile. "Power!" he said, shutting up one hand, his straight, fine features as hard as the cameo in his neckcloth.

She instantly fired at his tensity of will.

"How splendid you are, Alexander!" she cried. "How tremendously satisfactory for a woman to share! You can have no idea what it means to be with a man like a stone wall!

"I wish," she said, "that you would always tell me about your work. I'd like more than anything else to see you going on, step by step up. I suppose it is extraordinary in a woman. I felt that way about father's iron, and he only laughed at me; and yet once I kept a forge daybook almost a week, when a clerk was ill. I think I could be of real assistance to you, Alexander."

He regarded with the profoundest distaste any mingling of his, Alexander Hulings', wife and a commercial industry. He had married in order to give his life a final touch of elegance and proper symmetry. No, no; he wanted Gisela to receive him at the door of his mansion, in fleckless white, as she was now, and jewels, at the end of his day in the clamor and soot of business and put it temporarily from his thoughts.

He was distinctly annoyed that her father had permitted her to post the forge book; it was an exceedingly unladylike proceeding. He told her something of this in carefully chosen, deliberate words; and she listened quietly, but with a faint air of disappointment.

"I want you to buy yourself whatever you fancy," he continued; "nothing is too good for you—for my wife. I am very proud of you and insist on your making the best appearance, wherever we are. Next year, if the political weather clears at all, we'll go to Paris, and you can explore the mantua-makers there. You got the shawls in your dressing room?"

She hesitated, cutting uncertainly with a heavy silver knife at a crystallized citron.

Then, with an expression of determination, she addressed him again:

"But don't you see that it is your power, your success over men, that fascinates me; that first made me think of you? In a way this is not—not an ordinary affair of ours; I had other chances more commonplace, which my father encouraged, but they seemed so stupid that I couldn't entertain them. I love pretty clothes, Alexander; I adore the things you've given me; but will you mind my saying that that isn't what I married you for? I am sure you don't care for such details, for money itself, in the least. You are too strong. And that is why I did marry you, why I love to think about you, and what I want to follow, to admire and understand."

He was conscious of only a slight irritation at this masculine-sounding speech; he must have no hesitation in uprooting such ideas from his wife's thoughts; they detracted from her feminine charm, struck at the bottom of her duties, her privileges and place.

"At the next furnace in blast," he told her with admirable control, "the workmen will insist on your throwing in, as my bride, a slipper; and in that way you can help the charge."

Then, by planning an immediate trip with her to West Virginia, he abruptly brought the discussion to a close.

Alexander was pleased, during the weeks which followed, at the fact that she made no further reference to iron. She went about the house, gravely busy with its maintenance, as direct and efficient as he was in the larger realm. Almost her first act was to discharge the housekeeper. The woman came to Alexander, her fat face smeared with crying, and protested bitterly against the loss of a place she had filled since the house was roofed.

He was, of course, curt with her, and ratified Gisela's decision; but privately he was annoyed. He had not even intended his wife to discharge the practical duties of living—thinking of her as a suave figure languidly moving from parlor to dining room or boudoir; however, meeting her in a hall, energetically directing the dusting of a cornice, in a rare flash of perception he said nothing.

XII

HE would not admit, even to himself, that his material affairs were less satisfactory than they had been the year before, but such he vaguely knew was a fact. Speculation in Western government lands, large investments in transportation systems for the present fallow, had brought about a general condition of commercial unrest. Alexander Hulings felt this, not only by the delayed payment for shipments of metal, but in the allied interests he had accumulated. Merchandise was often preceded by demands for payment; the business of a nail manufactory he owned in Wheeling had been cut in half.

He could detect concern in the shrewd countenance and tones of Samuel Cryble, a hard-headed Yankee from a Scotch Protestant valley in New Hampshire, who had risen to the position of his chief assistant and, in a small way, copartner. They sat together in the dingy office on the public road and silently, grimly, went over invoices and payments, debts and debtors. It was on such an occasion that Alexander had word of the death of Doctor Veneada.

Hulings' involuntary concern, the stirred memories of the dead man's liberal spirit and mind—he had been the only person Alexander Hulings could call friend—speedily gave place to a growing anxiety as to how Veneada might have left his affairs. He had been largely a careless man in practical matters.

Alexander had never satisfied the mortgage he had granted Veneada on the timber properties purchased with the other man's money. He had tried to settle the indebtedness when it had first fallen due, but the doctor had begged him to let the money remain as it was.

"I'll only throw it away on some confounded soft-witted scheme, Alex," he had insisted. "With you, I know where it is; it's a good investment."

Now Hulings recalled that the second extension had expired only a few weeks before Veneada's death, incurring an obligation the settlement of which he had been impatiently deferring until he saw the other.

He had had a feeling that Veneada, with no near or highly regarded relatives, would will him the timber about the valleys; yet he was anxious to have the thing settled. The Alexander Hulings Company was short of available funds. He returned to Eastlake for Veneada's funeral; and there, for the first time, he saw the cousins to whom the doctor had occasionally and lightly alluded. They were, he decided, a lean and rapacious crew.

He remained in Eastlake for another twenty-four hours, but was forced to leave with nothing discovered; and it was not until a week later that, again in his office, he learned that Veneada had made no will. This, it seemed, had been shown beyond any doubt. He rose, walked to a dusty window, and gazed out unseeingly at an eddy of dead leaves and dry metallic snow in a bleak November wind.

After a vague, disconcerted moment he shrewdly divined exactly what would occur. He said nothing to Cryble, seated with his back toward him; and even Gisela looked with silent inquiry at his absorption throughout supper. She never questioned him now about any abstraction that might be concerned with affairs outside their pleasant life together.

The inevitable letter at last arrived, announcing the fact that, in a partition settlement of Veneada's estate by his heirs, it was necessary to settle the expired mortgage. It could not have come, he realized, at a more inconvenient time.

He was forced to discuss the position with Cryble; and the latter heard him to the end with a narrowed, searching vision.

"That money out of the business now might leave us on the bank," he asserted. "As I see it, there's but one thing to do—go over all the timber, judge what we actually will need for coaling, buy that—or, if we must, put another mortgage on it—and let the rest, a good two-thirds, go."

This, Alexander acknowledged to himself, was the logical if not the only course. And then John Wooddrop would purchase the remainder; he would have enough charcoal to keep up his local industries beyond his own life and another. All his—Alexander's—planning, aspirations, sacrifice, would have been for nothing. He would never, like John Wooddrop, be a great industrial despot, or command, as he had so often pictured, the iron situation of the state. To do that, he would have to control all the iron the fumes of whose manufacture stained the sky for miles about Harmony. If Wooddrop recovered an adequate fuel supply Alexander Hulings would never occupy a position of more than secondary importance.

There was a bare possibility of his retaining all the tracts again by a second mortgage; but as he examined that, it sank from a potentiality to a thing without substance. It would invite an investigation, a public gleaning of facts, that he must now avoid. His pride could not contemplate the publication of the undeniable truth—that what he had so laboriously built up stood on an insecure foundation.

"It is necessary," he said stiffly, "in order to realize on my calculations, that I continue to hold all the timber at present in my name."

"And that's where you make a misjudgment," Cryble declared, with an equal bluntness. "I can see clear enough that you are letting your personal feeling affect your business sense. There is room enough in Pennsylvania for both you and old Wood-drop. Anyhow, there's got to be somebody second in the parade, and that is a whole lot better than tail end."

Alexander Hillings nodded absently; Cryble's philosophy was correct for a clerk, an assistant, but Alexander Hillings felt the tyranny of a wider necessity. He wondered where he could get the money to satisfy the claim of the doctor's heirs. His manufacturing interests in West Virginia, depreciated as they were at present, would about cover the debt. Ordinarily they were worth a third more; and in ten years they would double in value. He relentlessly crushed all regret at parting with what was now his best property and promptly made arrangements to secure permanently the timberland.

Soon, he felt, John Wooddrop must feel the pinch of fuel shortage; and Alexander awaited such development with keen attention. As he had anticipated, when driving from the canal, he saw that the Blue Lump Furnace had gone out of blast, its workmen dispersed. Gisela, the day before, had been to see her father; and he was curious to hear what she might report. A feeling of coming triumph, of inevitable worldly expansion, settled comfortably over him, and he regarded his wife pleasantly through a curtain of cigar smoke.

They were seated in a parlor, already shadowy with an early February dusk; coals were burning brightly in a polished open stove, by which Gisela was embroidering in brightly colored wool on a frame. She had the intent, placid expression of a woman absorbed in a small, familiar duty. As he watched her Alexander Hulings' satisfaction deepened—young and fine and vigorous, she was preeminently a wife for his importance and position. She gazed at him vacantly, her eyes crinkled at the comers, her lips soundlessly counting stitches, and a faint smile rose to his lips.

He was anxious to hear what she might say about John Wooddrop, and yet a feeling of propriety restrained him from a direct question. He had not had a line, a word or message, from Wood-drop since he had married the other's daughter. The aging man, he knew, idolized Gisela; and her desertion—for so John Wooddrop would hold it—must have torn the Ironmaster. She had, however, been justified in her choice, he contentedly continued his train of thought. Gisela had everything a woman could wish for. He had been a thoughtful husband. Her clothes, of the most beautiful texture and design, were pinned with jewels; her deftly moving fingers flashed with rings; the symbol of his success, his——

"My father looks badly, Alexander," she said suddenly. "I wish you would see him, and that he would talk to you. But you won't and he won't. He is very nearly as stubborn as yourself. I wish you could make a move; after all, you are younger.... But then, you would make each other furious in a second." She sighed deeply.

"Has he shown any desire to see me?"

"No," she admitted. "You must know he thinks you married me only to get his furnaces; he is ridiculous about it—just as if you needed any more! He has been fuming and planning a hundred things since his charcoal has been getting low."

She stopped and scrutinized her embroidery, a naïve pattern of rose and urn and motto. He drew a long breath; that was the first tangible indication he had had of the working out of his planning, the justification of his sacrifice.

"I admire father," she went on once more, conversationally; "my love for you hasn't blinded me to his qualities. He has a surprising courage and vigor for an—— Why, he must be nearly seventy! And now he has the most extraordinary plan for what he calls 'getting the better of you.' He was as nice with me as possible, but I could see that he thinks you're lost this time.... No, the darker green. Alexander, don't you think the words would be sweet in magenta?"

"Well," he demanded harshly, leaning forward, "what is this plan?"

She looked up, surprised at his hard impatience.

"How queer you are! And that's your iron expression; you know it's expressly forbidden in the house, after hours. His plan? I'm certain there's no disloyalty in telling you. Isn't it mad, at his age? And it will cost him an outrageous amount of money. He is going to change the entire system of all his forges and furnaces. It seems stone coal has been found on his slopes; and he is going to blow in with that, and use a hot blast in his smelting."

Alexander Hulings sat rigid, motionless; the cigar in his hand cast up an unbroken blue ribbon of smoke. Twice he started to speak, to exclaim incredulously; but he uttered no sound. It seemed that all his planning had been utterly overthrown, ruined; in a manner which he—anyone—could not have foreseen. The blowing in of furnaces with hard coal had developed since his entrance into the iron field. It had not been generally declared successful; the pig produced had been so impure that, with working in an ordinary or even puddling forge, it had often to be subjected to a third, finery fire. But he had been conscious of a slow improvement in the newer working; he had vaguely acknowledged that sometime anthracite would displace charcoal for manufacturing purposes; in future years he might adopt it himself.

But John Wooddrop had done it before him; all the square miles of timber that he had acquired with such difficulty, that he had retained at the sacrifice of his best property, would be worthless. The greater part of it could not be teamed across Wooddrop's private roads or hauled advantageously over a hundred intervening streams and miles. It was all wasted, lapsed—his money and dreams!

"It will take over a year," she went on. "I don't understand it at all; but it seems that sending a hot blast into a furnace, instead of the cold, keeps the metal at a more even temperature. Father's so interested you'd think he was just starting out in life—though, really, he is an old man." She laughed. "Competition has been good for him."

All thrown away; in vain! Alexander Hulings wondered what acidulous comment Cryble would make. There were no coal deposits on his land, its nature forbade that; besides, he had no money to change the principal of his drafts. He gazed about at the luxury that surrounded Gisela and himself; there was no lien on the house, but there still remained some thousands of dollars to pay on the carpets and fixtures. His credit, at least, was unimpeachable; decorators, tradespeople of all sorts, had been glad to have him in their debt. But if any whisper of financial stringency escaped, a horde would be howling about his gate, demanding the settlement of their picayune accounts.

The twilight had deepened; the fire made a ruddy area in the gloom, into the heart of which he flung his cigar. His wife embroidered serenely. As he watched her, noting her firm, well-modeled features, realizing her utter unconsciousness of all that he essentially at that moment was, he felt a strange sensation of loneliness, of isolation.

Alexander Hulings had a sudden impulse to take her into his confidence; to explain everything to her—the disaster that had overtaken his project of ultimate power, the loss of the West Virginia interest, the tightness of money. He had a feeling that she would not be a negligible adviser—he had been a witness of her efficient management of his house—and he felt a craving for the sympathy she would instantly extend.

Alexander parted his lips to inform her of all that had occurred; but the habit of years, the innate fiber of his being, prevented. A wife, he reminded himself, a woman, had no part in the bitter struggle for existence; it was not becoming for her to mingle with the affairs of men. She should be purely a creature of elegance, of solace, and, dressed in India muslin or vaporous silk, ornament a divan, sing French or Italian songs at a piano. The other was manifestly improper.

This, illogically, made him irritable with Gisela; she appeared, contentedly sewing, a peculiarly useless appendage in his present stress of mind. He was glum again at supper, and afterward retired into an office he had had arranged on the ground floor of the mansion. There he got out a number of papers, accounts and pass books; but he spent little actual time on them. He sat back in his chair, with his head sunk low, and mind thronged with memories of the past, of his long, uphill struggle against oblivion and ill health.

Veneada was gone; yes, and Conrad Wishon too—the supporters and confidants of his beginning. He himself was fifty years old. At that age a man should be firmly established, successful, and not deviled by a thousand unexpected mishaps. By fifty a man's mind should be reasonably at rest, his accomplishment and future secure; yet there was nothing of security, but only combat, before him.

Wooddrop had been a rich man from the start, when he, Alexander Hulings, at the humiliating failure of the law, had had to face life with a few paltry hundreds. No wonder he had been obliged to contract debts, to enter into impossibly onerous agreements! Nothing but struggle ahead, a relentless continuation of the past years; and he had reached, passed, his prime!

There, for a day, he had thought himself safe, moving smoothly toward the highest pinnacles; when, without warning, at a few words casually pronounced over an embroidery frame, the entire fabric of his existence had been rent! It was not alone the fact of John Wooddrop's progressive spirit that he faced, but now a rapidly accumulating mass of difficulties. He was dully amazed at the treacherous shifting of life, at the unheralded change of apparently solid ground for quicksand.

XIII

THOUGH the industries centered in Tubal Cain were operated and apparently owned Cain by the Alexander Hulings Iron Company, and Hulings was publicly regarded as their proprietor, in reality his hold on them was hardly more than nominal. At the erection of the furnaces and supplementary forges he had been obliged to grant such rebates to the Columbus Transportation interest in return for capital, he had contracted to supply them at a minimum price such a large proportion of his possible output, that, with continuous shifts, he was barely able to dispose advantageously of a sixth of the year's manufacture.

He had made such agreements confident that he should ultimately control the Wooddrop furnaces; when, doubling his resources, he would soon free himself from conditions imposed on him by an early lack of funds. Now it was at least problematic whether he would ever extend his power to include the older man's domain. His marriage with Gisela had only further separated them, hardening John Wooddrop's resolve that Hulings should never fire a hearth of his, a determination strengthened by the rebuilding of Wooddrop's furnaces for a stone-coal heat.

The widespread land speculation, together with the variability of currency, now began seriously to depress the country, and, more especially, Alexander Hulings. He went to Philadelphia, to Washington, for conferences; but returned to his mansion and Gisela in an increasing someberness of mood. All the expedients suggested, the legalizing of foreign gold and silver, the gradual elimination of the smaller state-bank notes, an extra coinage, one after another failed in their purpose of stabilization; an acute panic was threatened.

Alexander was almost as spare of political comments to his wife as he was of business discussion. That, too, he thought, did not become the female poise. At times, bitter and brief, he condemned the Administration; during dinner he all but startled a servant into dropping a platter by the unexpected violence of a period hurled at the successful attempts to destroy the national bank. And when, as—he declared—a result of that, the state institutions refused specie payment, and a flood of rapidly depreciating paper struck at the base of commerce, Alexander gloomily informed Gisela that the country was being sold for a barrel of hard cider.

He had, with difficulty, a while before secured what had appeared to be an advantageous order from Virginia; and, after extraordinary effort, he had delivered the iron. But during the lapsing weeks, when the state banks refused to circulate gold, the rate of exchange for paper money fell so far that he lost all his calculated profit, and a quarter of the labor as well. The money of other states depreciated in Pennsylvania a third. In addition to these things

Alexander commenced to have trouble with his workmen—wages, too, had diminished, but their hours increased. Hulings, like other commercial operators, issued printed money of his own, good at the company store, useful in the immediate vicinity of Tubal Cain, but valueless at any distance. Cryble, as he had anticipated, recounted the triumph of John Wood-drop.

"The old man can't be beat!" he asserted. "We've got a nice little business here. Tailed on to Wooddrop's, we should do good; but you are running it into an iron wall. You ain't content with enough."

Cryble was apparently unconscious of the dangerous glitter that had come into Hulings' gaze. Alexander listened quietly until the other had finished, and then curtly released him from all connection, any obligation to himself. James Cryble was undisturbed.

"I was thinking myself about a move," he declared. "This concern is pointed bull-headed on to destruction! You're a sort of peacock," he further told Hulings; "you can't do much besides spread and admire your own feathers. But you'll get learned."

Alexander made no reply, and the other shortly after disappeared from his horizon. Cryble, he thought contemptuously, a man of routine, had no more salience than one of the thousands of identical iron pigs run from Glory Furnace. There commenced now a period of toil more bitter, more relentless, than his first experience in the valleys; by constant effort he was able to keep just ahead of the unprofitable labor for the Columbus Railroad. The number of workmen grew constantly smaller, vaguely contaminated by the unsettled period, while his necessity increased. Again and again he longed to strip off his coat and superfluous linen and join the men working the metal in the hearths; he would have felt better if he could have had actual part in rolling and stamping the pig beds, or even in dumping materials into the furnace stack.

In the fever of Alexander Hulings' impatience and concern, the manufacture of his iron seemed to require months between the crude ore and the finished bars and blooms. He detected a growing impotence among laborers, and told them of it with an unsparing, lashing tongue. A general hatred of him again flashed into being; but it was still accompanied by a respect amounting to fear.

He was approached, at a climax of misfortune, by representatives of the railroad. They sat, their solid faces rimmed in whiskers, and smooth fingers playing with portentous seals, in his office, while one of their number expounded their presence.

"It's only reasonable, Hulings," he stated suavely, "that one man can't stand up against present conditions. Big concerns all along the coast have gone to wreck. You are an exceptional man, one we would be glad to have in our

Company; and that, briefly, is what we have come to persuade you to do—to merge your activities here into the railroad; to get on the locomotive with us.

"Long ago you were shrewd enough to see that steam transportation was the coming power; and now—though for the moment we seem overextended—your judgment has been approved. It only remains for you to ratify your perspicacity and definitely join us. We can, I think, offer you something in full keeping with your ability—a vice presidency of the reorganized company and a substantial personal interest."

Alexander attended the speaker half absently, though he realized that probably he had arrived at the crisis of his life, his career; his attention was rapt away by dreams, memories. He saw himself again, saturated with sweat and grime, sitting with Conrad Wishon against the little house where they slept, and planning his empire of iron; he thought again, even further back, of the slough of anguish from which he had won free, and persistently, woven through the entire texture, was his vision of iron and of pride. He had sworn to himself that he would build success from the metal for which he had such a personal affinity; that he would be known as the great Ironmaster of Pennsylvania; and that unsubstantial ideal, tottering now on the edge of calamity, was still more potent, more persuasive, than the concrete and definite promises of safety, prosperity, the implied threat, of the established power before him.

He had an objective comprehension of the peril of his position, his negligible funds and decreasing credit, the men with accounts clamoring for settlement, he thought absurdly of a tessellated floor he had lately laid in his vestibule; the mingled aggression and uncertainty on every hand; but his subjective self rose up and dominated him. Louder than any warning was the cry, the necessity, for the vindication of the triumphant Alexander Hu-lings, perpetually rising higher. To surrender his iron now, to enter, a mere individual, however elevated, into a corporation, was to confess himself defeated, to tear down all the radiant images from which he had derived his reason for being.

Hulings thought momentarily of Gisela; he had, it might be, no right to involve her blindly in a downfall of the extent that now confronted him. However, he relentlessly repressed this consideration, together with a vague idea of discussing with her their—his—position. His was the judgment, the responsibility, that sustained them; she was only an ornament, the singer of little airs in the evening; the decoration, in embroidery and gilt flowers, of his table.

He thanked the speaker adequately and firmly voiced his refusal of the offer.

"I am an iron man," he stated in partial explanation; "as that I must sink or swim."

"Iron," another commented dryly, "is not noted for its floating properties."

"I am disappointed, Hulings," the first speaker acknowledged; "yes, and surprised. Of course we are not ignorant of the condition here; and you must also know that the company would like to control your furnaces. We have offered you the palm, and you must be willing to meet the consequences of your refusal. As I said, we'd like to have you too—energetic and capable; for, as the Bible reads, 'He that is not for me————'"

When they had gone, driving in a local surrey back to the canal, Alexander Hulings secured his hat and, dismissing his carriage, walked slowly down to Tubal Cain Forge. An increasing roar and uprush of sooty smoke and sparks marked the activity within; the water poured dripping under the water wheel, through the channel he had cleared, those long years back, with bleeding hands; strange men stood at the shed opening; but the stream and its banks were exactly as he had first seen them.

His life seemed to have swung in a circle from that former day to now—from dilemma to dilemma. What, after all, did he have, except an increasing weariness of years, that he had lacked then? He thought, with a grim smile, that he might find in his safe nine hundred dollars. All his other possessions suddenly took on an unsubstantial aspect; they were his; they existed; yet they eluded his realization, brought him none of the satisfaction of an object, a fact, solidly grasped.

His name, as he had planned, had grown considerable in men's ears, its murmur rose like an incense to his pride; yet, underneath, it gave him no satisfaction. It gave him no satisfaction because it carried no conviction of security, no personal corroboration of the mere sound.

What, he now saw, he had struggled to establish was a good opinion in his own eyes, that actually he was a strong man; the outer response, upon which he had been intent, was unimportant compared with the other. And in the latter he had not moved forward a step; if he had widened his sphere he had tacitly accepted heavier responsibilities—undischarged. A flicker hammered on a resonant limb, just as it had long ago. How vast, eternal, life was! Conrad Wishon, with his great arched chest and knotted arms, had gone into obliterating earth.

Death was preferable to ruin, to the concerted gibes of little men, the forgetfulness of big; once, looking at his greying countenance in a mirror, he had realized that it would be easier for him to die than fail. Then, with a sudden twisting of his thoughts, his mind rested on Gisela, his wife. He told himself, with justifiable pride, that she had been content with him; Gisela was not an ordinary woman, she had not married him for a cheap and material reason, and whatever admiration she had had in the beginning he had been able to preserve. Alexander Hulings was certain of that; he saw it in a hundred little acts of her daily living. She thought he was a big man, a successful man; he had not permitted a whisper of his difficulties to fret her serenity, and, by heaven, he thought with a sharp return of his native vigor, she never should hear of them; he would stifle them quietly, alone, one by one.

The idea of death, self-inflicted, a flaccid surrender, receded before the flood of his returning pride, confidence. Age, he felt, had not impaired him; if his importance was now but a shell, he would fill it with the iron of actuality; he would place himself and Gisela for ever beyond the threats of accident and circumstance.

XIV

GISELA had been to Philadelphia, and she was unusually gay, communicative; she was dressed in lavender-and-rose net, with black velvet, and about her throat she wore a sparkling pendant that he had never before noticed.

"I hope you'll like it," she said, fingering the diamonds; "the shape was so graceful that I couldn't resist. And you are so generous, Alexander!"

He was always glad, he told her briefly, to see her in new and fine adornments. He repressed an involuntary grimace at the thought of the probable cost of the ornament. She could hardly have chosen a worse time in which to buy jewels. Not only his own situation, but the whole time, was one for retrenchment. The impulse to tell her this was speedily lost in his pride of her really splendid appearance. He himself had commanded her to purchase whatever she fancied; he had explained that that—the domain of beauty—was exclusively hers; and it was impossible to complain at her first considerable essay.

Here his feeling was rooted in the deepest part of his being—he was, after all, twenty-five years older than Gisela; and, as if in a species of reparation for the discrepancy, he owed her all the luxury possible. This he had promised her—and himself; and an inability to provide gowns and necklaces and gewgaws was a most humiliating confession of failure, a failure unendurable to him on every plane. Alexander, too, had told her finally that she had no place in his affairs of business; and after that he could not very well burden her with the details of a stupid—and momentary—need for economy.

"I got a sweet bouquet holder," she continued; "in chased gold, with garnets. And a new prayer book; you must see that—bound in carved ivory, from Paris." He listened with a stolid face to her recital, vaguely wondering how much she had spent; how long the jeweler would wait for settlement. "And there was a wonderful Swiss watch I thought of for you; it rang the hours and———"

"That," he said hastily, "I don't need. I have two excellent watches."

"But you are always complaining!" she returned, mildly surprised. "I didn't get it, but told the man to put it aside. I'll write if you don't want it."

"Do!"

Suddenly he felt weary, a twinge of sciatica shot through his hip; he must keep out of the damp cast houses, with their expanses of wet sand. But actually he was as good as he had ever been; better, for he now saw clearly what he must accomplish, satisfy. The present national crisis would lift; there was already a talk of the resumption of gold payment by the state banks; and the collapse of a firm associated with him in a rolling mill had thrown its control into his hands. Steam power had already been connected, and he could supply the railroad corporation with a certain number of finished rails direct, adding slightly to his profit.

The smallest gain was important, a scrap of wood to keep him temporarily afloat on disturbed waters; he saw before him, close by, solid land. But meantime more than one metaphorical wave swept over his head, leaving him shaken. The Columbus people returned a shipment of iron, with the complaint that it was below the grade useful for their purpose. He inspected the rejected bars with his head forgeman, and they were unable to discover the deficiency.

"That's good puddled iron," the forgeman asserted. "I saw the pig myself, and it could have been wrought on a cold anvil. Do they expect blister steel?"

Alexander Hulings kept to himself the knowledge that this was the beginning of an assault upon his integrity, his name and possessions. At court he could have established the quality of his iron, forced the railroad to accept it within their contract. But he had no money to expend on tedious legal processes; and they knew that in the city.

"We can get a better price for it than theirs," he commented.

The difficulty lay in supplying a stated amount. The forgeman profanely explained something of his troubles with labor:

"I get my own anvils busy, and perhaps the furnaces running out the metal, when the damn charcoal burners lay down. That's the hardest crowd of niggers and drunken Dutch that ever cut wood! It's never a week but one is shot or has his throat cut; and some of the coal they send down looks like pine ash."

At their home he found Gisela with the draperies of the dining room in a silken pile on the carpet.

"I'm tired of this room," she announced; "it's too—too heavy. Those plum-colored curtains almost made me weep. Now what do you think? A white marble mantel in place of that black, and a mirror with wreaths of colored gilt. An apple green carpet, with pink satin at the windows, draped with India muslin, and gold cords, and Spanish mahogany furniture—that's so much lighter than this." She studied the interior seriously. "Less ormolu and more crystal," Gisela decided.

He said nothing; he had given her the house—it was her world, to do with as she pleased. The decorating of the dining room had cost over three thousand dollars. "And a big Chinese cage, full of finches and rollers." He got a certain grim entertainment from the accumulating details of her planning. Certainly it would be impossible to find anywhere a wife more unconscious of the sordid details of commerce. Gisela was his ideal of elegance and propriety.

Nevertheless, he felt an odd, illogical loneliness fastening on him here, where he had thought to be most completely at ease. His mind, filled with the practical difficulties of tomorrow, rebelled against the restriction placed on it; he wanted to unburden himself of his troubles, to lighten them with discussion, give them the support of another's belief in his ability, his destiny; but, with Cryble gone, and his wife dedicated to purely aesthetic considerations, there was no one to whom he dared confess his growing predicament.

Marriage, he even thought, was something of a failure—burdensome. Gisela, in the exclusive rôle of a finch in an elaborate cage, annoyed him now by her continual chirping song. He thought disparagingly of all women; light creatures fashioned of silks and perfume; extravagant. After supper he went directly into his office room.

There, conversely, he was irritated with the accounts spread perpetually before him, the announcements of fresh failures, depreciated money and bonds. He tramped back and forth across the limited space, longing to share Gisela's tranquillity. In a manner he had been unjust to her; he had seen, noted, other women—his own was vastly superior. Particularly she was truthful, there was no subterfuge, pretense, about her; and she had courage, but, John Wooddrop's daughter, she would have. Alexander Hulings thought of the old man with reluctant admiration; he was strong; though he, Hulings, was stronger. He would, he calculated brutally, last longer; and in the end he would, must, win.

XV

YET adverse circumstances closed about him like the stone walls of a cell. The slightest error or miscalculation would bring ruin crashing about his pretensions. It was now principally his commanding interest in the rolling mill that kept him going; his forges and furnaces, short of workmen, were steadily losing ground. And, though summer was at an end, Gisela chose this time to divert the labor of a considerable shift to the setting of new masoned flower beds. He watched the operation somberly from the entrance of the conservatory attached, like a parti-colored fantastic glass bubble, to his house.

"It won't take them over four or five days," Gisela said at his shoulder.

He positively struggled to condemn her foolish waste, but not a word escaped the barrier of his pride. Once started, he would have to explain the entire precarious situation to her—the labor shortage, the dangerous tension of his credit, the inimical powers anxious to absorb his industry, the fact that he was a potential failure. He wished, at any sacrifice, to keep the last from his wife, convinced as she was of his success.

Surely in a few months the sky would clear and he would triumph—this time solidly, beyond all assault. He rehearsed this without his usual conviction; the letters from the Columbus System were growing more dictatorial; he had received a covertly insolent communication from an insignificant tool works.

The Columbus Railroad had written that they were now able to secure a rail, satisfactory for their purpose and tests, at a considerably lower figure than he demanded. This puzzled him; knowing intimately the whole iron situation, he realized that it was impossible for any firm to make a legitimate profit at a smaller price than his. When he learned that the new contracts were being met by John Wooddrop his face was ugly—the older man, at a sacrifice, was deliberately, coldly hastening his downfall. But he abandoned this unpleasant thought when, later, in a circuitous manner, he learned that the Wooddrop Rolling Mills, situated ten miles south of the valleys, were running on a new, secret, and vastly economical system.

He looked up, his brow scored, from his desk. Conrad Wishon's son, a huge bulk, was looking out through a window, completely blocking off the light. Alexander Hulings said:

"I'd give a thousand dollars to know something of that process!"

The second Wishon turned on his heel.

"What's that?" he demanded.

Alexander told him. The other was thoughtful.

"I wouldn't have a chance hereabouts," he pronounced; "but I'm not so well known at the South Mills. Perhaps———"

Hulings repeated moodily:

"A thousand dollars!"

He was skeptical of Wishon's ability to learn anything of the new milling. It had to do obscurely with the return of the bars through the rollers without having to be constantly re-fed. Such a scheme would cut forty men from the pay books.

A black depression settled over him, as tangible as soot; he felt physically weary, sick. Alexander fingered an accumulation of bills; one, he saw, was from the Philadelphia jeweler—a fresh extravagance of Gisela's. But glancing hastily at its items, he was puzzled—"Resetting diamond necklace in pendant, fifty-five dollars." It was addressed to Gisela; its presence here, on his desk, was an error. After a momentary, fretful conjecturing he dismissed it from his thoughts; women were beyond comprehension.

He had now, from the sciatica, a permanent limp; a cane had ceased to be merely ornamental. A hundred small details, falling wrongly, rubbed on the raw of his dejection. The feeling of loneliness deepened about him. As the sun sank, throwing up over, the world a last dripping bath of red-gold light, he returned slowly to his house.

Each window, facing him, flashed in a broad sheet of blinding radiance, a callous illumination. A peacock, another of Gisela's late extravagances, spread a burnished metallic plumage, with a grating cry.

But the hall was pleasantly still, dim. He stood for a long minute, resting, drawing deep breaths of quietude. Every light was lit in the reception room, where he found his wife, seated, in burnt-orange satin and bare powdered shoulders, amid a glitter of glass prisms, gilt and marble. Her very brilliance, her gay, careless smile, added to his fatigue. Suddenly he thought—I am an old man with a young wife! His dejection changed to bitterness. Gisela said:

"I hope you like my dress; it came from Vienna, and was wickedly expensive. Really I ought to wear sapphires with it; I rather think I'll get them. Diamonds look like glass with orange." Her words were lost in a confused blurring of his mind. He swayed slightly. Suddenly the whole circumstance of his living, of Gisela's babbling, became unendurable. His pride, his conception of a wife set in luxury above the facts of existence, a mere symbol of his importance and wealth, crumbled, stripping him of all pretense. He raised a thin, darkly veined and trembling hand.

"Sapphires!" he cried shrilly. "Why, next week we'll be lucky if we can buy bread! I am practically smashed—smashed at fifty and more. This house that you fix up and fix up, that dress and the diamonds and clocks, and—and——They are not real; in no time they'll go, fade away like smoke, leave me, us, bare. For five years I have been fighting for my life; and now I'm losing; everything is slipping out of my hands. While you talk of sapphires; you build bedamned gardens with the men I need to keep us alive; and peacocks and——"

He stopped as abruptly as he had commenced, flooded with shame at the fact that he stood before her self-condemned; that she, Gisela, saw in him a sham. He miserably avoided her gaze, and was surprised when she spoke, in an unperturbed warm voice:

"Sit down, Alexander; you are tired and excited." She rose and, with a steady hand, forced him into a chair. "I am glad that, at last, you told me this," she continued evenly; "for now we can face it, arrange, together. It can't be so bad as you suppose. Naturally you are worn, but you are a very strong man; I have great faith in you."

He gazed at her in growing wonderment; here was an entirely different woman from the Gisela who had chattered about Viennese gowns. He noted, with a renewed sense of security, the firmness of her lips, her level, unfaltering gaze. He had had an unformulated conviction that in crises women wrung their hands, fainted. She gesticulated toward the elaborate furnishings, including her satin array:

"However it may have seemed, I don't care a bawbee about these things! I never did; and it always annoyed father as it annoyed you. I am sorry, if you like. But at last we understand each other. We can live, fight, intelligently."

Gisela knew; regret, pretense, were useless now, and curiously in that knowledge she seemed to come closer to him; he had a new sense of her actuality. Yet that evening she not only refused to listen to any serious statements, but played and sang the most frothy Italian songs.

XVI

ON the day following he felt generally upheld. His old sense of power, of domination, his contempt for petty men and competitions, returned. He determined to go to Pittsburgh himself and study the labor conditions; perhaps secure a fresh, advantageous connection. He was planning the details of this when a man he knew only slightly, by sight, as connected with the coaling, swung unceremoniously into his office.

"Mr. Hulings, sir," he stammered, "Wishon has been shot—killed."

"Impossible!" he ejaculated.

But instantly Alexander Hulings was convinced that it was true. His momentary confidence, vigor, receded before the piling adversities, bent apparently upon his destruction.

"Yes, his body is coming up now. All we know is, a watchman saw him standing at a window of the Wooddrop Mills after hours, and shot him for trespassing—spying on their process." Alexander's first thought was not of the man just killed, but of old Conrad, longer dead. He had been a faithful, an invaluable, assistant; without him Hulings would never have risen. And now he had been the cause of his son's death! A sharp regret seized him, but he grew rapidly calm before the excitement of the inferior before him.

"Keep this quiet for the moment," he commanded.

"Quiet!" the other cried. "It's already known all over the mountains. Wishon's workmen have quit coaling. They swear they will get Wood-drop's superintendent and hang him."

"Where are they?" Hulings demanded.

The other became sullen, uncommunicative. "We want to pay them for this," he muttered. "No better man lived than Wishon."

Alexander at once told his wife of the accident. She was still surprisingly contained, though pale. "Our men must be controlled," she asserted. "No further horrors!"

Her attitude, he thought, was exactly right; it was neither callous nor hysterical. He was willing to assume the burden of his responsibilities. It was an ugly, a regrettable, occurrence; but men had been killed in his employ before—not a week passed without an accident, and if he lost his head in a welter of sentimentality he might as well shut down at once. Some men lived, struggled upward. It was a primary part of the business of success to keep alive.

Gisela had correctly found the real danger of their position—the thing must go no further. The sky had clouded and a cold rain commenced to fall. He could, however, pay no attention to the weather; he rose from a partial dinner and departed on a score of complicated and difficult errands. But his main concern, to locate and dominate the mobbing charcoal burners, evaded his straining efforts. He caught rumors, echoed threats; once he almost overtook them; yet, with scouts placed, they avoided him.

He sent an urgent message to John Wooddrop, and, uncertain of its delivery, himself drove in search of the other; but Wooddrop was out somewhere in his wide holdings; the superintendent could not be located. A sense of an implacable fatality hung over him; every chance turned against him, mocked the insecurity of his boasted position, deepened the abyss waiting for his suspended fall.

He returned finally, baffled and weary, to his house; yet still tense with the spirit of angry combat. A species of fatalism now enveloped him in the conviction that he had reached the zenith of his misfortunes; if he could survive the present day.... A stableman met him at the veranda.

"Mrs. Hulings has gone," the servant told him. "A man came looking for you. It seems they had Wooddrop's manager back in the Mills tract and were going to string him up. But you couldn't be found. Mrs. Hulings, she went to stop it."

An inky cloud floated nauseously before his eyes—not himself alone, but Gisela, dragged into the dark whirlpool gathered about his destiny! He was momentarily stunned, with twitching hands and a riven, haggard face, remembering the sodden brutality of the men he had seen in the smoke of charring, isolated stacks; and then a sharp energy seized him.

"How long back?" Hulings demanded.

"An hour or more, perhaps a couple."

Alexander raged at the mischance that had sent Gisela on such an errand. Nothing, he felt, with Wooddrop's manager secured, would halt the charcoal burners' revenge of Wishon's death. The rain now beat down in a heavy diagonal pour, and twilight was gathering.

"We must go at once for Mrs. Hulings," he said. Then he saw Gisela approaching, accompanied by a small knot of men. She walked directly up to him, her crinoline soggy with rain, her hair plastered on her brow; but her deathly pallor drove everything else from his observation. She shuddered slowly, her skirt dripping ceaselessly about her on the sod.

"I was too late!" she said in a dull voice. "They had done it!" She covered her eyes, moved back from the men beside her, from him. "Swinging a little... all alone! So sudden—there, before me!" A violent shivering seized her.

"Come," Alexander Hulings said hoarsely; "you must get out of the wet. Warm things. Immediately!"

He called imperatively for Gisela's maid, and together they assisted her up to her room. Above, Gisela had a long, violent chill; and he sent a wagon for the doctor at Harmony.

The doctor arrived, and mounted the stairs; but, half an hour later, he would say little. Alexander Hulings commanded him to remain in the house. The lines deepened momentarily on the former's countenance; he saw himself unexpectedly in a shadowy pier glass, and stood for a long while subconsciously surveying the lean, grizzled countenance that followed his gaze out of the immaterial depths. "Alexander Hulings," he said aloud, in a tormented mockery; "the master of—of life!" He was busy with the local marshal when the doctor summoned him from the office.

"Your wife," the other curtly informed him, "has developed pneumonia."

Hulings steadied himself with a hand against a wall.

"Pneumonia!" he repeated, to no one in particular. "Send again for John Wooddrop."

He was seated, a narrow, rigid figure, waiting for the older man, in the midst of gorgeous upholstery. Two facts hammered with equal persistence on his numbed brain: one that all his projects, his dream of power, of iron, now approached ruin, and the other that Gisela had pneumonia. It was a dreadful thing that she had come on in the Mills tract! The Columbus System must triumphantly absorb all that he had, that he was to be. Gisela had been chilled to the bone; pneumonia! It became difficult and then impossible to distinguish one from the other—Gisela and the iron were inexplicably welded in the poised catastrophe of his ambition.

Alexander Hulings rose, his thin lips pinched, his eyes mere sparks, his body tense, as if he were confronting the embodied force that had checked him. He stood upright, so still that he might have been cast in the metal that had formed his vision of power, holding an unquailing mien. His inextinguishable pride cloaked him in a final contempt for all that life, that fate, might do. Then his rigidity was assaulted by John Wooddrop's heavy and hurried entrance into the room.

Hulings briefly repeated the doctor's pronouncement Wooddrop's face was darkly pouched, his unremoved hat a mere wet film, and he left muddy exact footprints wherever he stepped on the velvet carpet.

"By heaven!" he quavered, his arms upraised.

"If between us we have killed her——" His voice abruptly expired.

As Alexander Hulings watched him the old man's countenance grew livid, his jaw dropped; he was at the point of falling. He gasped, his hands beating the air; then the unnatural color receded, words became distinguishable: "Gisela!... Never be forgiven! Hellish!" It was as if Death had touched John Wooddrop on the shoulder, dragging a scarifying hand across his face, and then briefly, capriciously, withdrawn.

"Hulings! Hulings," he articulated, sinking weakly on a chair, "we must save her. And, anyhow, God knows we were blind!" He peered out of suffused rheumy eyes at Alexander, appalling in his sudden disintegration under shock and the weight of his years. "I'm done!" he said tremulously. "And there's a good bit to see to—patent lawyer tomorrow, and English shipments. Swore I'd keep you from it." He held out a hand, "But there's Gisela, brought down between us now, and—and iron's colder than a daughter, a wife. We'd best cover up the past quick as we can!"

At the instant of grasping John Wooddrop's hand Alexander Hulings' inchoate emotion shifted to a vast realization, blotting out all else from his mind. In the control of the immense Wooddrop resources he was beyond, above, all competition, all danger. What he had fought for, persistently dreamed, had at last come about—he was the greatest Ironmaster of the state!

Milton Keynes UK
Ingram Content Group UK Ltd.
UKHW030912151124
451262UK00006B/793